Maxine stood in the doorway, a silhouette, leaning against the wooden wall inside the car. The box behind her was empty and dark. She'd been lucky this time — the last boxcar, all hers. *Lucky. Humph.* She allowed herself a small grin. Six months now. She pulled at the binding that cut under her arms and wrinkled her nose at the smell. The fabric of the overalls she'd stolen from a clothesline rubbed between her ˙ thighs and she grimaced. *Six months and I've not yet gotten used to that* . . . Six months of being Max, just another guy on the road.

Florida was hot and getting hotter as summer settled in, dragging on into days that never seemed to end, wavering over the shining rails, but she'd heard there was work in Tampa, cigar factory work, and she figured if it was factory, she could do it. Maybe save up enough to sleep someplace other than a flop. Maybe be a girl again. Maybe be visible again. *Maybe go home.* "No," she said softly and shook her head. "No."

The train slowed for a town of small gray wood houses with tilting porches and dirt yards. Church bells. *Must be Sunday.* Maxine looked out and ahead, along the side of the train. A figure in pants and holding a long stick jumped from a boxcar ahead just as the train crossed the main dirt road of the town. He stumbled — not a regular hobo, Maxine thought — and sat down hard in the dust. A hat rolled away as Maxine's car passed, and she saw long brown hair unfurl. *A girl!*

About the Author

Teresa Stores currently lives in Vermont and teaches at local colleges. This is her second novel.

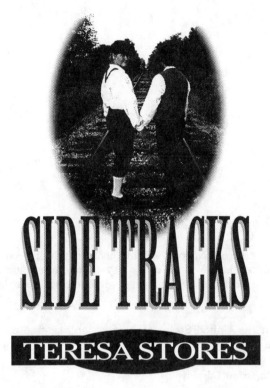

SIDE TRACKS

TERESA STORES

THE NAIAD PRESS, INC.
1996

Printed in the United States of America on acid-free paper
First Edition

Editor: Christine Cassidy
Cover designer: Bonnie Liss (Phoenix Graphics)
Typesetter: Sandi Stancil

Library of Congress Cataloging-in-Publication Data

Stores, Teresa, 1958 –
    Side tracks / by Teresa Stores.
        p.   cm.
    ISBN 1-56280-122-8 (pbk.)
    1. Depression—United States—Fiction. 2. Lesbians—United
States—Fiction. 3. Tramps—United States—Fiction. I. Title.
PS3569.T6486S53   1996
813'.54—dc20   95-39252
                                                                        CIP

Dedicated to:

*Damien, who wanted to be a ballerina with toe
shoes and tutu
David, who wanted to be a missionary nurse with a
little white hat
John, who wanted to be McMillan's Wife with hot
pants and go-go boots
Felice, who wanted to be a lion tamer with a whip
and a chair
Susan, who wanted to be Superman with red tights
and a cape
Jenny, who wanted to be a dinosaur
Susan, who wanted to be a mailbox*

*to the little girls who wanted to grow up to be boys,
to the little boys who wanted to grow up to be girls,
and
to all those who have become others.*

Acknowledgments

The original idea and much of the historical background for this book came from *Boxcar Bertha: An Autobiography, as told to Dr. Ben L. Reitman* (1937; reprint, New York, Amok Press, 1988). *Hard Times: An Oral History of the Great Depression,* by Studs Terkel (New York, Random House, 1970, 1986) and *Odd Girls and Twilight Lovers: A History of Lesbian Life in Twentieth Century America,* by Lillian Faderman (New York, Penguin Books, 1992) were also excellent historical resources, and no work based in lesbian history can fail to acknowledge the fantastic collection at the New York Lesbian Herstory Archives. For challenging me to question my own definitions and ideas about gender and otherness, I must thank Kate Bornstein (*Gender Outlaw: On Men, Women, and the Rest of Us,* New York, Routledge, 1994) and my friend and odd twin, Jenny Hubbard. As always, I thank my publisher, Barbara Grier, for her patience and support, and my editor, Christine Cassidy, for her precision and insight. Dierdre O'Neille and Susan Jarvis are my dedicated cheerleaders and critical first readers, and I thank them for always being there, always believing, always loving.

The sound is that of a shaggy death, a stuttering *sh-sh-sh*-shearing away of that which obscures — and that which marks — to a ragged edge. It is the sound of a boat slicing through a choppy lake, of boots crossing coarse sand, an invisible boundary, to some other land . . . Canada or Mexico, the moon. It is a whispering rip of farewell, a distant locomotive's call.

It's only hair.

Maxine forced herself to look in the mirror. Her eyes, blue ringed in black, pupils large in the candlelight, were watery. *Blink, damn it.* She blinked fast, swallowed and shook her head. At her right temple, the orange hair stood out straight and short,

1

prickly even. She almost laughed, then choked and sniffed the tears back in.

Come on, you have to.

She grabbed another handful of hair and watched her trembling hand raise the scissors. Firming her jaw and clenching her teeth, Maxine watched the silver shears close, listening again to the sound of parting, then looked for a second at the reddish golden strands, as long as her arm, and let them fall to the floor.

Maxine McCarthy had never cut her hair. None o' that flapper, modern-girl fashion for Mick McCarthy's girl. She liked taking the motor bus downtown, though, to watch those other women, those folks who lived in Greenwich Village. And it wasn't just the hair, the clothes — the women who wore pants, the fine men with bright ties and thin mustaches who greeted each other with kisses on the street, and the women with dresses cut high above the knee, low at the neck — no, it was something about the way they led their lives, different from everybody else, that fascinated Maxine. *Not that I'd ever want to be like them* . . . She shivered at the cool shears against her neck and blinked. It made Maxine afraid to think of being so different . . . so obvious . . .

She thought of her father — stepfather — staggering into the table, swearing at the crash of it, reeking of hooch, his face and fists red, and of the little ones behind her mother's skirts, the deep lines in her mother's forehead, the white strands in her mother's own long red hair. *And she's not yet thirty-five.* Last night . . . *Every night* . . . Maxine sighed, tired with the effort of pretending they were like everyone else, wondering how much the neighbors heard through the walls. *Ordinary, why can't I be ordinary?*

Maxine focused on her face in the mirror. She touched the cool scissors to the blue bruise swelling her cheekbone. Warm tears collected at the blades. It seemed like she couldn't ever be invisible enough anymore. She lifted her chin. *No more.* The El train shook the building as it passed, and she looked up, inhaled a deep breath, and set her backbone straight.

She pushed the scissors through her hair again, close to her head, a wide swath this time. The blades closed and the veil fell away, brushing her bare shoulder in a prickling, sweeping hush. She watched her head appearing — rounder, wider than she expected — as if curtains were parting on stage. *An actor.*

A train whistle blew, farther away, in the freight yards this time, hollow and yearning, a cry like that of the geese Maxine so loved to watch in November, long vee's of dark flight, escape from the cold, the ugly city winter, a cry of leaving. Her throat and nose filled suddenly. *Such a sad sound.* I'll be gone before the geese return, she thought, and tried to smile, holding back her tears.

A rustle behind her. She froze and watched in the mirror as one of the lumps in the bed rolled to the side. The other children were still: four of them together under the thin blanket. Patrick, the one who had rolled over, began to breathe deep again. He'll have my bed, she thought. He'd be twelve soon, already big, stocky like his father. He'd have to go alone to the factory from now on, without his big sister. They'd fired her because she was a girl. "Plenty of men with families need work," the foreman had said, and somebody had to be let go. Patrick was of use, still young, big. *A boy.* He'd keep bringing money home. *Time he had his own bed.* Mama wanted her to go to Cousin Nat up North. She said maybe he could get her work in the mills there, or in his shop, but Maxine remembered the way the man had watched her, his little eyes following her wherever she moved. *Time to disappear.*

A breeze brushed a stray strand of hair from her neck, and she shivered. Her body was pale; it seemed to fade already from the room. The pink of her nipples, aroused by the breeze, seemed darker, rosy and distant, rising from the swell of her breasts. She frowned into her reflection, lifted her hands and pushed her breasts in. They weren't so large for a girl of seventeen, but still . . .

Maxine pulled a cotton scarf from a nail and wound it tight around her breasts, binding them down, smoothing the flatness. She would miss the way they rounded her shape, the soft roll she had begun to notice in her shoulders as she walked. *A boy, play the part of a boy.* She buttoned up one of her stepfather's shirts, stolen when she did the laundry yesterday, over the binding, and pulled Patrick's knickers up by the suspenders, leaving them loose at her waist. The rough fabric rubbed her thighs between her legs. Something to get used to, she thought. She stepped back from the small, clouded mirror, closed her eyes and opened them. *A boy.*

The red hair was uneven . . . a cowlick? The figure was not tall, not short. A small freckled nose. The clothes were rough and mended and the shoes scuffed. Nearly invisible lashes, a black ring around

4

the startling blue of the eyes. Maybe 15 or 16. Irish. *Not much to look at, but a boy.* Maxine tried to grin at her reflection but bit her lip instead.

Another train rumbled by and the floorboards vibrated through her shoes, up her thighs. She walked to the bed, silent, and pulled the blanket higher over the shoulders of the three little girls, the big little boy. She thought for a moment of her mother and felt the wrenching in her throat like a saw against metal bars. They'll manage without me, she thought. *I have to go.*

She tucked the handkerchief with the almost two dollars Mama had been saving to send her to Lowell — to Cousin Nat — into the binding under her shirt. She reached down for the neatly rolled and rope-tied blanket that held her other socks, the penknife she had found in the gutter, the loaf of bread from the Italian bakery, the can of beans she had taken from the pantry.

A lock of her golden-red hair lay draped across the bedroll. She picked it up, a silky soft lump, and fingered the strands like tiny lines, minute threads unraveling, dividing them between her fingers. The hairs fell silently away. *I am gone.*

The scream of the train whistle wandered out across the gently unfolding green of Central Florida hills, along the brown-needled floor of the sweet piney woods, under the drooping moss-draped live oaks, down into the dark mud bogs, tripping lightly over soft cypress knees. Random bits of train song — track clack, whistle and steam harmony, groan and squeak of weight and wood and iron — brushed the brows of children rubbing their dusty shoes against their calves, tickled the soles of men with lines etched deep in leathery brows as they tucked their collars down to hide frayed edges and straightened their ties. Women looked up, tugging their slips, and away into the air where the train song lingered for a second before the biscuits burning or the pastor's greeting called them back. The train lumbered heavy, growling and snorting, a curling dark line, and its song meandered, sad, thrilling, an indiscriminate version of love, into the nooks and crannies and hidden places where ordinary people lived.

One of them sat in the open door of the boxcar, her head tilted to listen, green eyes unfocused as the pine trees in rows and lines flashed past, drawing in on a stained cigarette, blowing a blue haze out to be swept behind in the draft. The rough shoes and dirty overall-clad legs swung in and out with the rhythm of riding. The cane fishing pole sticking out the door rattled. She looked up at the early blue sky, tucked a stray brown lock of hair back under her man's hat and grinned.

I, Josephine Lee, am not an ordinary one.

The whistle called again, and her heart jerked against her ribs, longing. The train lurched as it began to slow. Holding her hat — her brother Jack's hat — Jo looked out the boxcar door and up the side of the train. *Signpost ahead.* She scrambled to her feet, flicked away her cigarette butt and grabbed the fishing pole, ready to jump. She touched her pocket, the envelope there, for reassurance.

"Nothin' left for the ordinary guy," Bert shouted over the rumble of the train. The boxcar acted as a drum, amplifying the train noise, and in the dim light from the half-opened door, some of the half-dozen men sprawled about the floor cocked their heads or cupped their hands to their ears to hear better. Most just ignored him. He took a swig from the bottle passed to him and rubbed the scratchy growth of whiskers on his chin. "Ain't nothin' left," he yelled, "and suits me fine." He grinned, settling back against the wall. "They're all against the ordinary guy. Roosevelt, Hoover, the whole bunch of 'em." The whiskey dribbled down his chin as the train lurched. He wiped the liquor off and then sucked the back of his hand clean. "Ordinary guy ain't got nothin' anymore."

Maxine stood in the doorway, a silhouette, leaning against the wooden wall inside the car. The box behind her was empty and dark. She'd been lucky this time — the last boxcar, all hers. *Lucky. Humph.* She allowed herself a small grin. Six months now. She pulled at the binding that cut under her arms and wrinkled her nose at the smell. The fabric of the overalls she'd stolen from a clothesline rubbed between her thighs and she grimaced. *Six months and I've not yet gotten used to that.*

Six months of being Max, just another guy on the road. She scratched her head, the prickly hairs of her latest jungle haircut. Felt kind of uneven, but it didn't really matter. Nobody much looked at her, at least she hoped not. She tried not to be noticed anyway. *Safer that way.* And it wasn't hard to be invisible these days. Lots of folks were invisible, lots of folks a blur, trying not to be noticed, trying not to notice themselves. Maxine sighed, watching the pine trees in neat rows flash past.

Florida was hot and getting hotter as summer

settled in, dragging on into days that never seemed to end, wavering over the shining rails, but she'd heard there was work in Tampa, cigar factory work, and she figured if it was factory, she could do it. Maybe save up enough to sleep someplace other than a flop. Maybe be a girl again. Maybe be visible again. *Maybe go home.* "No," she said softly and shook her head. "No."

The train slowed for a town of small gray wood houses with tilting porches and dirt yards. Church bells. *Must be Sunday.* Maxine looked out and ahead, along the side of the train. A figure in pants and holding a long stick jumped from a boxcar ahead just as the train crossed the main dirt road of the town. He stumbled — not a regular hobo, Maxine thought — and sat down hard in the dust. A hat rolled away as Maxine's car passed, and she saw long brown hair unfurl. *A girl!* Green eyes met hers, and she leaned out as the train began to pick up speed, pulling away, but it was too late to get a clearer look at the face. *But, a girl.*

Jo felt the gaze harder than the bruise on her rear. The boy's eyes were blue, almost bluer than the still lake on a Sunday morning. She sat in the middle of Main Street, dusty all over, her hair a mess. He leaned out to keep watching her as the train rolled south away from her, and his red hair was a bright contrast against the dark interior of the boxcar behind him. *He was lucky, going somewhere.* Josephine felt her hand lifting of its own accord and felt the warmth of a blush rising up her neck at the same moment. The boy, leaning out far now, hesitated a second, and then he waved. She watched the orange spot of his head diminish.

The street was suddenly quiet without the train, and slowly the sounds of the mockingbird and the church bells penetrated. Josephine's head snapped around. *Dang!* She jumped to her feet, grabbed the fishing pole and hat and raced toward the parsonage next to the neat white church. *Gotta get changed.* The bells were angry. *Dang!*

The church was straight white lines, no shadows, no ornament. There were no doubts about this building, no trees in the church yard, no chips in the white paint. It sat square in the center of its square lot, so clear, so sharp and stark in the bright Florida sun that it hurt the eyes. It did not invite except that it seemed simple, solid, safe.

Jo pulled the heavy door open as slowly and silently as she could, watching her white-gloved hand on the handle. It was smudged already, and she knew she still smelled faintly of fish. She heard her father's voice, steady and deep, the closing prayer. *Dang. Really late.* She pushed the door a bit more open, holding her breath.

"...and we thank thee, oh Lord, for bringin'" these families here today to be one with Your family...one with the family of God. We ask Your blessing on th —"

The door handle slipped out of her glove. Jo reached in for it, stepping up. Her Bible fell with a soft flutter and thud. The door thumped open against the wall. She looked up as Pastor Lee — *Father* — opened his eyes.

"...Your blessing upon this house of the Lord," he prayed, glaring at his daughter, who stood disheveled and stiff in the open sanctuary door, "and upon these dear children..." An angry note bit into the last word as he ground it out from his clenched jaw.

Josephine felt the heat of a blush rush up her neck and bent to pick up her Bible. *I'm going to get it after church.* The skirt of her dress caught on the doorknob, and silently struggling to free herself, she cursed it. The *skerrrch* as it ripped caused more than one head to turn, and Jo's face burned again as she pulled the door shut and straightened her skirt.

"...of God. We beg Your mercy," Pastor Lee went on, looking hard at her as she walked as quietly as she could toward the family pew at the front. "...on those who stray, oh Lord!" her father nearly shouted.

As Josephine passed the bowed heads, a few people glanced up. Some folks just grinned, eyes still closed. Rafe looked up and winked, but Jo pretended not to see.

"...and Your bountiful blessing of faith in the mysteries of Thy way for the shepherds of Your

flock." He sighed. Jo felt a small twinge. *Mysteries?*
He never talks about mysteries.

"You are the great Father; we humble ourselves
before You," he continued. Jack, Josephine's twin,
slid over as she reached their pew. "It is in Your
name we pray," he finished, sounding tired. "Amen."
His eyes flashed out across the congregation at his
daughter again.

Josephine looked over at her mother, but the
powdered-soft cheeks and brow were stiff; she stared
straight ahead. Kate and Willy grinned unabashedly
at their big sister until Mrs. Lee gave them both
sharp elbow pokes, and they settled back on her
either side. Jack kept his green eyes on the front of
the church, but they twinkled, creasing at the
corners, and a note appeared out of his hand and
dropped into Jo's lap. She opened it: "Catch any?"
She grinned.

"You missed Daddy's sermon on 'honor thy
mother and father,'" Jack said. He shifted the
stringer of bream and his cane pole to his other
hand, blew out a haze of smoke from the cigarette
between his teeth, and passed it over to his sister,
striding beside him, a bit shorter, in identical clothes.

The neat rows of pines on each side of the two-
track dirt road stretched out into shadowy tunnels.
Jo looked down the darkness, as she always did, for
pink and white wild dogwoods and plums between
the rows in the spring, soft brown bunnies or the
white flash of a deer's tail. A red cardinal, eyes

13

bright through his mask, flashed from the woods, perched just ahead and began to bark out his cheep-cheep. She shook her head. "I've heard it before."

Jack laughed. "And you'll hear it again pretty soon, I'd bet."

"Yeah." Jo laughed too, glancing over at her tall, thick brother. "And I'll have hell to pay if he figures out I'm not in my room right now." The pants she had borrowed from him were cuffed up and belted tight, and his shirt would drag around her knees had she not cut it off and tucked it in. He took long slow strides, and Jo lengthened her own, matching his gait and the swing of his shoulders. Except for size and her long hair, and the parts hidden under clothes, they looked the same — hair the brown of acorns, eyes as green as the pines overhead, lashes that curled long and dark. "Wasted on a boy," their mom always said. She'd pitch a fit to see me dressed in his clothes, Jo thought. Why, we even hold our cigarettes the same. She inhaled and grinned to herself, looking down at the weeds growing between the sandy ruts.

Jack took a last drag and tossed his cigarette into the woods. Josephine felt her head tilt in reflex to the whistle of a train approaching and smiled. It echoed between the piney lines and blurred in the shadows. A pale moon glowed in the distant curve between dark rows against a blue sky like a ghost or an angel.

"Guess I'm not much of a preacher's kid." She sighed. Or much of a girl, either.

Jack clapped a big hand on her shoulder. "Aw, Daddy'll forget everything when you and Rafe get married, Sis."

His hand was warm, but heavy. She pushed it away. "What if I don't want to marry Rafe?" she muttered. *What if I don't want to spend my whole life taking care of some man, having his kids, washing his socks, cleaning his house in this slow little town?*

Jack shrugged his head. "You'll marry somebody else then. Daddy don't care. Long as he's a church boy." He looked at her sideways. "So what's wrong with Rafe?"

Josephine scuffed her brown shoes into the dirt. She kicked the head off a dandelion. Something empty — or something extra, she couldn't tell which — floated through the walls that divided her organs inside. *Dang. Why wasn't I born a boy?* She shook her head. "Dang, Jack, I don't know. Maybe it's something wrong with me."

The train rumbled through the woods just off the road and out of sight, and she glanced toward the sound. Its smoke rose in dark blotches against the blue sky. "Every girl in town is crazy for Rafe," Jack coaxed.

Jo sighed again. "He says he loves me." She thought of the young man's grin, the way they'd been pals, the three of them, since they'd been kids, fishing and hunting and building treehouses in the woods. And now, Rafe's suddenly fervent way of trying to catch her hand, talk seriously and sweetly to her, and the curious hollow that opened up inside her when he did. *What does a boy, a man, feel?* She shuddered. It was as if he didn't even really see her anymore.

The smoke hung, dissipating, as the train noise faded. "I don't know," she said. "I guess I just don't love him."

"Aw, love's a crock," said Bert.

He was drunk. They all were. Warily, Maxine sat with her back to the wall beside the door of the side-tracked boxcar and watched the men playing cards.

"Some damn woman thought up love to trap a fella down. Women's for to screw and get the hell out." Bert slapped down his card and rubbed his chin. He glanced up at Maxine. "Right, young fella? Ya don't want ta get tied down afore ya seen the world, eh?"

Maxine didn't like the way he always eyed her, even when he was drunk, squinting. She was just another one of the guys now, but this Bert fellow looked at her as if he could see through the clothes and cropped hair. *And it makes him mad.* "Yeah, sure Bert," she answered.

Bert grinned, his eyes narrow. He gestured at her with his cigar. "Max here's a cagey one. He ain't got ta worry 'bout gettin' caught. New Yawk boy."

The other men laughed. The half dozen or so were all sizes, all ages, all colors of skin. Some wore parts of suits, and some were nearly in rags. All were dirty. The boxcar stank.

One man — he looked about her stepfather's

age — dressed in a suit, maybe once a businessman, his hair grown shaggy, greasy, and streaked with gray, his eyes lined and red, spoke quietly, sadly. "I had a family once." The others kept their eyes turned away. Maxine saw one man bite his lip and a young boy blinking fast. "It was kind of nice," he said.

"Hah!" Bert scoffed and took a swig from his bottle. "No freedom." He looked around at the lowered heads. He waved the bottle at Maxine. "Not like this 'un. 'Where ya goin'?' I axed young Max, and he says, 'Nowhere, just goin'.'" Bert grinned, his teeth brown and the corners of his mouth cracked and gooey. Maxine looked down. "Now that's the kind to be. No home. No fambly. Just goin'."

Maxine looked out the door of the boxcar and inhaled deeply and slowly. The men behind her slapped cards and smoked. The sun was setting beyond the trees. *Family. Home.* She blinked the tears back and swallowed. *Just goin'.*

Josephine climbed carefully from the oak onto the roof of the porch and then crept up the slope, over the shingles, to her bedroom window. The sun was just going down, a huge orange *O* just above the trees. From here she could see a glint on the lake where she and Jack had fished all afternoon. She put her legs in her window and scooted in under the curtain.

"Oh, Josephine." Her mother stood in the doorway, Father just behind her, with her hand over her mouth and her eyes wide and hurt.

"How could you do this to your mother?" Father

shouted in his sermon voice. "Women are to adorn themselves in modest apparel!" His face was red and his neck bulged out over his stiff white collar. He pointed his long index finger at Jo. "This is obscene!"

"What if someone had seen you?" Mother whispered from behind her hand.

Jo felt a twinge of guilt. "It's just pants," she said, shrugging. "Women up North —"

"Hussies," Father hissed. "No Christian woman —"

"Oh my." Jo's mother leaned back against the doorframe. She seemed even smaller than before.

"See what you've done to your mother?" He looked down his nose at Jo.

"I'm sorry," she said.

"You're always sorry," he shouted, almost before she could get the words out. "Sorry doesn't make you any less an embarrassment. Sorry doesn't help your mother hold her head up in this town. Sorry doesn't —"

"So let me leave," Jo said softly, meeting his eyes.

Mother sank into the chair beside the door, ignoring Jo's Sunday dress heaped there. "Leave?" she said faintly.

Jo knelt beside her mother. "See, Mama." She pulled the worn letters from her pocket. "Miss Langley wrote away to her friend up North . . . Miss Langley wants me to go to college, Mama, see?" The words stumbled over one another in her rush to get them out. "Miss Langley and her friend Miss Corwin wrote for me to go to their college up North." Her mother took off Jo's hat and began to comb through her long hair with her fingers. "It's a college for girls, Mama," Jo said. The words seemed to be

18

bunched in her chest, crowding out. She held the
letter in her mother's lap. "Miss Corwin will sponsor
me, Mama. They want me. See? I can go there,
Mama."

"Waste of money!" Father spluttered. "Miss
Langley," he spat out. "That old maid never had a
lick of sense." He scowled at his wife. "I told you
sending her to that school was a waste. Some rich
woman putting highfalutin' ideas in girls' heads . . .
Education is a waste on a girl," he said to Jo. "I'm
just a poor country preacher. I can't be spending
money on you to go to some fancy college just so you
can teach in some fancy school like Miss Langley's
for a year or two before you get a man and babies."

Jo jumped to her feet and drew her shoulders
back. "But Miss Corwin and Miss Langley are going
to pay for me, Father," she said, her voice rising.
"And I won't —"

"Won't what?" he shouted. He made himself taller
than her and pushed his body forward. "Won't get
married?" He snorted a laugh. "No, you won't, if you
dress like that! No man'll have you."

"Maybe I don't want a man, Father." Jo felt her
tongue moving and cringed, but she couldn't stop the
words. *Maybe I just want to find my way on my own.*
Her mother drew in a sharp breath. Father's eyes
bulged. "I'm not like other girls," she whispered.

"You are certainly a mystery to me, Josephine
Lee." Father sighed, his breath hard and warm. "The
good Lord knows I've tried."

Jo blinked. I am a mystery to me, she thought.
She looked down at her mother. Help me, she
thought, meeting her eyes.

"Why can't you be satisfied with being like

everyone else?" Her mother's voice wavered. "We have a responsibility before God, Jo," she pleaded. "To be examples . . . honest, plain, good."

"This is honest," Jo said softly, gesturing to her clothes, the letter in her mother's hands. "This is part of who I am."

Father threw up his hands and paced down the hall and back. Her mother looked down at the papers in her lap again, and Jo thought she saw a twitch at her mouth. But it was gone when the older woman looked up and blinked, her gaze shifting to her husband.

"Mama?"

"Silence!" The preacher's voice thundered. "That's enough! You will stay in this house until you move into your husband's house. That is the way of the good Christian woman. I make the rules in this house, and if you will not obey, then you are no daughter of mine." His gray eyes had glazed over, cold, and his face had settled into rigid lines. He spun on his heel and strode from Jo's room.

His wife's gaze followed him down the hall. Jo dropped again to the floor beside her mother's knees. "Mama?" She looked down at the weave of the cotton in her mother's dress, uneven squares, overlapping threads. She touched the soft folded hands.

Mama sighed. "'Let the woman learn in silence with all subjection,'" she began to recite. Jo looked up, not breathing. Mama's eyes were wet, and Jo knew she would cry in a minute. She took Jo's hand in hers and squeezed. "You are a smart girl, Josephine, and I'm right proud of you." The screen door slammed downstairs. Her face hardened. "What makes you think you'll fit in in a fancy girl's college like that, Jo?"

Josephine felt her heart shrinking, her chest closing in. She looked down. "I don't belong here, Mama," she murmured.

Mama held Jo's hand tighter. "You just don't try hard enough," she said. "You're a pretty girl, Josephine. We let you go to Miss Langley's so you would learn to be more ladylike and —"

"But . . ." Jo started.

Mama frowned, her eyebrows and mouth thin fences, curving down. " 'I permit not a woman to teach, nor to usurp authority over the man, but to be in silence,' " Mama finished, sadly. "First Timothy."

"You should stand up to him, Mama," Jo said. Her voice sounded hard, strong. "Women don't have to take that anymore, Mama." *What's wrong with her?*

Jo felt the tears well in her own eyes, and she watched her mother's hands draw away from her own. "He's right, Josephine. You'll find a good man — maybe Rafe — and all this won't mean anything anymore." She paused. "You've got to stop thinking life is like them movies you watch down at the Savoy. There's the real life and there's dreaming, and it's time you knew the difference." She stood up, leaving Jo on her knees beside the chair. Folding the letters carefully, Mama put them on the dressing table and turned to leave. "He's my husband, Josephine," she said, pausing in the doorway. She looked small and squashed and lonely, Jo thought, like the marigolds planted between the garden rows of vegetables to keep the bugs away. "The good book says, 'Wives submit to your husbands,' " Mama said. "It's the Lord's way, honey. You'll see." Her hand lifted as if to touch Jo's head, then fell back to her side lifeless again, empty. "You'll fall in love, like I did, and none of this will matter anymore."

Jo watched her mother's shoes follow the lines of wood floor down the hallway. A tear — glassy, silver — splattered, a dark spot, beside her knee.

The hair fell in a long dark wave to the floor. Jo watched her hand, Mama's good sewing scissors glittering in the moonlight, her face serious and hard in the mirror. She cut another strand and caught it in her hand. Brown and long and straight, it draped a good six inches over each side of her palm. *A woman's glory, the Bible says.* She put it carefully on the dressing table, then lifted another lock, cut it and placed it with the other. Methodically, Jo worked her way around her head — lifting, watching the silver blades separate and close with a smooth whisper, placing the hair on the brown heap — until it was Jack's face she saw in the mirror. *A boy.* She grinned Jack's grin at herself. *"Her hair is given her for a covering," it says.* She ran her hand through the soft shaggy bowl of her new haircut, her disguise. *Not uncovered . . . covered.* She caught her reflection, eyes wide for a second, green, the long lashes. *Wasted on a boy.* She grinned again.

The bundle of hair was silky and fine and, like a small soft animal, it kept trying to slip from her hands as she tied a blue ribbon around it. Jo put it in the fold of the letter to Mama. She stuffed another, a single lock, into her knapsack, safe with the papers from Miss Carlotta Corwin, New York City, and the onion-skin map, neatly folded, the way north through places she didn't know, yet. The money went into the wrap around her breasts and she glanced up, her heart thudding faster, as a train whistle called "Hell-oooo" through the night.

The moon reflected through the open window over her shoulder in the mirror, and Jo touched her hair again. "... and the head of the woman is the man ..." Serious green eyes looked into her. *What am I now?*

The full moon overflowed a clear gray light through the oaks and cypress and moss. It was swollen with possibility, a belly pregnant with the yellow lunacy of anything might happen. Shadows made its face arch up in eyebrows, mouth a round *O,* questioning, waiting for something to happen.

Maxine leaned from the open door of the boxcar and stretched her eyes up the tracks of the siding, where the moonlight gleamed in two straight, safe lines. North. *Toward home.*

The men behind her were very drunk now, laughing until they choked. Bert's eyes were on her back again. She could feel him watching her. *Anything might happen.*

Maxine thought about the jobs in Tampa. *Probably nothing there, really.* She'd followed dozens of rumors up and down the rails with the hundreds of other fellows, hungry for work, hungry for a home. Everybody was looking, good regular people with nothing left but the clothes on their backs. Everybody wandering, and nothing out there anywhere — no jobs, no home. *Nothing, no place for me out there.*

Bert's voice growled something low in the hollow boxcar, and the men snorted, chuckled with a dark sound. Maxine's stomach clenched. The moonlight pulled at her feet like a tide. She was tired. It seemed as if she never slept, always alert for something, waiting for something, hoping to find something. *Nothing, no place for me out here on the road.* She thought again of her home, her mother and the children, and of Mick McCarthy's red fists and his anger. Of Cousin Nat and his small eyes. She glanced back into the dark. *But I don't belong here either.* Bert bent his head close to the other men in a tight circle, talking. She cocked her head, but the only voices she could make out were a mockingbird in the night, her own heart humming.

Moving slowly, Maxie jumped down from the boxcar. The soft thud felt good, the earth jolting into her bones. No one inside looked up. She reached back in and grabbed her roll of things. A cool, swampy breeze lifted the hairs on her arms and at the back of her neck. She smiled. She tugged at the binding that dug into her armpits and wished again she didn't need the disguise. The moon wavered as a cloud washed its edges, then swelled back out again.

Maxine turned north, walking along the silvery rails toward the main tracks. *Home.* She felt the moon at her back and watched her long shadow flickering across the black ties, as if climbing a ladder. The wind snickered in the pine trees and a faraway train whistle howled. Maxine stepped up to balance lightly on the moonlit rail. *Anything might happen.*

Jo glanced down the tracks to see the light of the freight train slow for Main Street. The parsonage, across the tracks, and the even lines of the white church were quiet, dull in the light from the moon. Her feet itched. She felt something rustling in her chest, like something wild in the underbrush. The train seemed to rumble up through the ground, through her shoes, into her bones. It passed between her and the houses, slow and loud and heavy. Jo laughed as she reached up for a rung on a boxcar and her feet lifted, swinging into the air like a dancer's, from Main Street. She settled into a sit, her feet dangling from the open boxcar door, grinning into the questioning face of the full moon. *Going, moon.* She spoke aloud, "Going places, moon." *Gone.*

"Come on you! Keep up!"
Jo started awake. The morning was still. Birds chirped outside. The train wasn't moving.
"Come on, I said!" The man's voice was rough, coming closer. Jo sat up and scrambled closer to the wall near the open door of the car, dragging her pack behind.

"Hey, pal. Come on . . ." A second man's voice, whining. "Give me a break this time." She heard the footsteps stop a couple of cars away.

Jo held her breath and peered out slowly.

A man in a uniform was looking into a boxcar, a pistol in one hand and another man handcuffed to his other wrist. The prisoner was scruffy and unshaven, steel gray hair standing up every which way, yawning. *A hobo and an agent.*

"Yeah, yeah," the voice from the boxcar said, "that's what you guys all want, a break." The hobo stopped in mid-yawn and his eyes went wide as he saw Jo. "Bunch a' worthless bums," the agent continued. "Still sleepin' at ten in the mornin'." The hobo grinned at Jo, then winked. The agent looking into the boxcar began to draw back out. "That's all the break you deserve."

Jo pulled her head back inside quickly and slipped her knapsack over her shoulders, listening, staring into the uneven lines of light seeping in through the cracks in the wooden walls.

"Ah, come on," the hobo said. "I'm on my way up North to get a job. I'm a workin' man too."

The gravel crunched closer. "Sure, sure, buddy," said the agent. "And I'm the King of England. I let you off and you'll tell all the other hoboes between here and Chicago about the soft touch in Starke, Florida. 'Fore I know it, I'll have bums lined up waitin' to get in the yard." Jo heard the agent's voice echo hollowly inside the boxcar next to hers.

"Oh yeah," the other man said, a bit louder than necessary. "I'll be tellin' all my buddies to hide just inside the boxcars and jump out and yell 'boo,' so's you can invite them home for tea and crumpets too."

Jo grinned. Ah, my cue, she thought. *Nice fellow.* She tensed into a crouch just inside the square light of the open door. The gravel crunched just outside.

"Wouldn't the missus love that..." the agent began, his shadow falling across the light.

"Boo!" Jo burst into his face so close she could smell the coffee on his breath and see the color drain from his lips.

"Aaaa!" He started back, and the hobo handcuffed to his wrist jerked him off his feet. They both fell into the dirt, and Jo jumped from the boxcar and ran for the woods, her legs pumping, her heart thudding.

"You, boy!" the agent shouted. She thought she heard a shot, but it was far behind her and wild into the air. When she reached the cool shade of the woods, she slowed to a trot, easing into the shadows, and realized her face was wide, the shape of a grin. Free, she thought. *I'm a boy and I'm free.*

The heat was a demon, an imp lolling fat and heavy on his back, hands folded on his belly, breathing slow, dense cumulus clouds, crushing the flat of North Florida. The cicadas chugged a tired, deliberate *idge-idge-idge* in the earthy-sweet plots of peanuts, cotton, beans. Nothing moved. Railroad ties sweated black, steaming up, the silver tracks whitening, and fat rattlesnakes stretched out across them, limp with the luxury of sun.

Joan of Arc, Joan of Arc. Jo walked as slowly as she could, watching the weeds and the tracks on either side for snakes, forcing her dusty shoes to keep lifting and setting down. No train had passed all day. Her shirt was soaked, the binding underneath melting into her skin. She felt cool trickles gather into rivers and course down the shadowy crease between her small breasts. She took off her hat and let the air cool through the short damp hair. She ruffled it with her palm, grinning. The heat flickered up from the railroad ties, and she thought of her favorite movie, her heroine. The name marched in her head in time with the crunching gravel under her feet, a chant: *Joan of Arc, Joan of Arc.*

Farmland stretched out around her, tended in some plots, gone to weeds and saplings in others. Occasionally an empty house, boarded up, blank-faced, would remind her of the hard times, the folks who had disappeared, the empty pews in her father's church. Daddy had preached on the Beatitudes once last year.

"Blessed are the poor in spirit," he'd read quietly, sadly, from the pulpit, "for theirs is the kingdom of heaven." He talked about hope and faith and living right, honesty . . . *honesty* . . . but there had been some-thing hollow — even to Jo with her neat clothes and full stomach and Miss Langley's School for Girls — something empty in her father's voice, sifting up into the rafters and white spaces of the church, when he'd finished. "Rejoice, and be exceedingly glad; for great is your reward in heaven . . ." There were folks who couldn't feed their children, who'd been foreclosed by the bank, sitting in the pews around her, and Jo had shifted uncomfortably on the wooden seat, wishing her father had some more immediate reward to offer.

Jo stopped as she spotted a small snake between the black ties, its diamond-shaped head waving back and forth, tasting the air for her movement. Her brother Jack or her father would've killed it, simple and quick, but she skirted wide around the little rattler, lifting her pack to cool her sweaty back for a second, thinking of Joan of Arc in the fire, then trudged on, smiling grimly to herself. " 'Blessed are ye when men shall revile you, and persecute you,' little snake," she muttered. *I really don't understand God sometimes.*

Something down there. The fishing line between her thumb and index finger twitched almost imperceptibly. Jo watched the brown water far below, moving slowly under her dangling feet. She sat perfectly still, but her stomach grumbled. *Come on, you fat old lazy bass.* The air was heavy but a barely cooler draft seeped up between the ties of the trestle, shaded by oaks leaning in from the riverbanks. The St. Marys River, according to her map. *Dividing line.* Georgia was just on the other side. The tree frogs had begun to scream for rain. The fish bumped the bait again. *Take it, dang it.*

She felt a thin vibration suddenly, in the small of her back where it touched the metal rail. The line in her hand jerked hard. *Dang.* Jo looked from the brown water to the place where the tracks curved into the woods beyond the bridge and then back to the water again. She scrambled to her feet, trying to pull up on the fishing line. She heard the train rumble. She looked back at the trees, shrugging her pack over a shoulder. The bass at the end of her line struggled. The whistle screamed, close. *Too close.* Jo let the fishing line go and began to step quickly from black tie to black tie across the bridge. *Twenty yards, ten.* She glanced back.

The snout of the train shoved around the curve, and the grate of the cowcatcher grinned wickedly. The trestle began to shake under her. The whistle shrieked, a banshee laugh. Jo felt her heart crash into her throat. *Run.* Jo ran.

The ties jumped under her feet. She watched her knees pumping, her shoes magically touching down on the black wooden lines, missing the cracks, seeming wider than they really were, where, far below, the brown water slogged along. She could feel the hot breath of the engine panting at her back. The bank lay ahead, three steps to red clay, two . . . The scream burst out of the thick thunder of iron and Jo threw herself off the tracks into the weeds.

She rolled down the bank a few feet and lay watching the huge round metal wheels and the underbelly of the freight cars, gasping the furnace blast of air into her lungs. *North.* The train was going north. Jo sat up. She looked back along the trestle; the boxcars were still pouring out of the woods. *Not all that fast.* She scrambled to her feet.

When the train curved into the shade, Maxine sat up and crossed her legs, stretched her arms wide and yawned. The wind from the open door became slightly cooler, and she scooted closer to look out into the green. A river, brown and sluggish, appeared underneath, and Maxine admired the way the moss trailed from the oak trees into the water, stirring little swirls. She wondered where they were, then shrugged. *As long as I'm headed somewhere I might belong.*

The train rumble deepened again as it left the bridge, and Maxine glanced out and ahead. A boy was jogging alongside the train. He glanced up at the side of the boxcar.

Maxie didn't think. She reached toward him, her arm long and bare and thin. He looked up, saw her and grinned. *Green eyes, long lashes.* Maxine stretched as far as she could, but the train was too fast, he was too slow. Their fingertips brushed.

He lunged forward, stumbled, then stopped in his tracks. Maxine stood up in the doorway and leaned out to look back, her hand prickling from the boy's touch. He lifted his shoulders in a shrug, palms up and mouthed an "oh, well." Maxine grinned back. *Oh well.*

The boxcar was a womb, thick with the smell of oranges, close and warm, creaking as it swayed around the bends, tracks cracking below in a deep bass, the rhythm of a rocking chair over a loose porch board. It was an ungentle cradle, not at all womanly, but angled and sharp, crates stacked in teetering rows, swaying wooden cages of green-yellow fruit, ripening in the dark. Something bumped the wooden wall.

Jo sat up fast, shaking her head to clear the sticky strings of sleep. A hand appeared at the cracked-open door of the boxcar. The train swayed, slowly rounding a bend. Another hand, the partner of the first, reached in and flattened out on the floor of the car. A man's head appeared, bent, and then his shoulders. He hoisted one leg up.

The man scrambled in, breathing hard, sat up and looked around. *The hobo in the handcuffs.* "Well," he grinned broadly, a brown front tooth half gone, "if it ain't my old friend, Boo." Jo ran a hand through her short hair and glanced down. "Shall we head on back to have some tea and crumpets, Boo?" The hobo laughed.

Jo smiled, but she could feel the skin pulling across her cheekbones, stiff. "Uh, yeah," she said, then stopped and gave herself a little shake. *Voice lower.* "Yeah, sure," she croaked.

The man studied her, the dirty lines in his forehead creasing in a frown. Jo stiffened more. *Does he see a boy or a girl?*

"Friendly young feller, ain't ya?" He stood up and reached out his hand. "Name's Bert."

Jo recoiled despite herself, away from the black-lined nails and the man's stink, the black edge of his shadow.

He snorted, a rough mean sound, pulling his hand back and settling into a nook between orange crates. "Reckon I am lookin' pretty scary these days."

Wake up! Jo shook herself and met Bert's eyes. They were bloodshot. "Uh, sorry," she said. "I'm, uh, Joe. Pleased to meet you."

Bert grinned and mimicked her. " 'Pleased ta meetcha!' " he sing-songed. "Ain't been on the road long, have ya?" He laughed.

The warmth of a blush spread up Jo's back and cheeks, and she was glad for the dirt of traveling and darkness of the boxcar. She shrugged. "Not too long."

"Cuz, no offense, but you ain't learned nothin' 'bout bein' one a us. Got ta stick together, ya know."

What does he want? Jo stuttered, "Uh, I, I . . . uh, thanks for helping me get away from that agent."

Bert snorted. "Don't thank me for nothin'." His voice was hoarse, gritty and too loud. Jo tried to watch him without staring. "That's what I mean by bein' one a us. I woulda done it for any fella . . ." He glanced at her sideways. "And they woulda done it for me."

Jo tried to let her back relax some. He seemed harmless enough, though his stench nearly overpowered the smell of oranges. The train whistle settled back over their car, and then farther back and off into the night, and Jo wondered, was there any more beautiful sound? She rolled the stiffness out of her shoulders and tried to smile at the hobo. "I didn't mean any offense."

Bert laughed heartily, sputtering. "Ah, don't worry about it kid." He reached into his shirt and pulled out a bottle. "Have a drink with me and we'll call ourselves pals."

Liquor. Father would kill me. Jo hesitated. She and Jack had found a still once in the woods, and she'd spied on the joint down by the river sometimes, the men and women laughing loudly, the piano's songs drifting out over the water. They'd all seemed so happy. *Free.* But it was the devil's work, Father always said.

"Come on, kid," Bert said, "be a man."

Jo grinned in spite of herself. *A man.* She reached

for the bottle Bert held toward her. It smelled of kerosene, but she wiped off the mouth carefully with her shirttail, Bert chuckling as he watched, and took a swig. The sides of her mouth caved in and the liquid ate into her throat. She choked. Bert burst out laughing again.

"Ain't much of a drinker, are ya, boy?"

Jo gasped the air. The alcohol burned down her pipes and spread warmth into her chest. She felt her shoulders loosen. She blinked and took another swig. "It's my Father who isn't . . . ain't much of a drinkin' man," she said, "not me." Jo passed the bottle back and grinned. "Thanks, Bert."

He snorted, and Jo noticed that he didn't seem so threatening anymore. The sharp sound of his nails scratching the stubble on his chin was dull, almost soothing. He smiled more slowly, and Jo's eyes fixed on the gap where his tooth was broken. "Quite welcome, Joe," Bert said softly. He settled back against the orange crates and yawned. "Now where ya say you're headed, pal?" he asked.

Jo reached for the bottle he held out to her. It seemed to sway in the air a little. It took a second of concentration to grab it from his hand. She felt happy, warm. Sleepy. "North," Jo said, smiling to herself. She took a swallow from the bottle, and this time it stretched out along her legs and arms like the sun radiating up from a warm wood floor. "Like you, Bert, goin' North." Her tongue was thicker now, heavy. The bottle slipped as she passed it back, but Bert caught it before it fell.

He laughed. "Oh hell, kid, I was just sayin' that to butter up that dumb agent. It don't matter where I'm goin'. I'm just goin'. Just goin'." He leaned back, and Jo could see his eyes watching her through thin slits. She felt her own lids drooping lower.

Jo heard the bottle thunk softly as Bert set it on the floor of the boxcar. The jerks and bumps of the train seemed softer now, rolling like quiet waves. Jo's head tilted toward her shoulder, and she heard Bert's voice far away. "Just goin'."

Jo rolled, dreaming she was in a boat. Waves pounded against the hull next to her head. Loud. Inside her head. "Uhhhnnhhh." The sound of her groan thudded against her eye sockets. She was all alone in a little wooden boat. Salt spray. *Gray*. Where was everyone? *Where am I going?* She licked her lips.

The train rounded another bend and as she began to roll again, she opened her eyes. "Uhhn." She squinted at the thin cracks of light through the wooden slats of the boxcar walls. They seemed to slice into her head. Her forehead's slow fog began to dissipate. *Bert.*

Jo rolled her head slowly to the side. *Gone.* A green blur through the open door. "Ohhhuhhhh." As her stomach flipped over, Jo lunged for the door. She closed her eyes to the dizzying flashes of ground and track while her insides heaved. She gripped the door frame. It was as if a fist clinched the back of her head when she turned over, gasping. Jo looked up at the ceiling. "Lord, Father was right." She grinned, then winced. "It's the work of the devil."

The canvas of her pack brushed her face, and Jo reached up for it. *Open.* She sat up fast. "Uhhn." Her skull seemed to cave in. She closed her eyes and rested for a minute, the flashes of light behind her lids swirling. Finally, she looked again.

The pack was open. Her extra shirt lay over there in the hay with her map. The lock of her hair tied in the blue ribbon . . . Jo picked it up and smoothed the long silky strands until they were neat. A cool breeze touched her neck, her chest. *What?* Jo looked down, suddenly afraid. *God.* Her shirt was open, the white cloth of her binding bright under the faded blue of her shirt, Jack's shirt. She hesitated, remembering her tough, gentle twin. No one had ever bothered her with him around.

The money was gone. She knew it was gone before she reached into the strip of cloth and between her small breasts. *Dang.* She lowered her chin to her knees. *Bert knows.* Her stomach twisted again at the thought of his hands there. Jo swallowed hard. She couldn't remember anything. *But my clothes are still on.* Her hand touched her belt. *Still tight.*

The soft lock of hair brushed her wrist. *Mama has the lock I left, tied just like this. She must worry.* The memory of Jo's room came rushing back to her: the quilt she and Mama pieced, the cedar chest — her hope chest — Father and Jack had made, the white curtains blowing out the open window, the oak tree just outside . . . the one she used to climb down to get out, to get away, *to go . . .*

Jo sighed. Wrapping her arms tighter around her knees and wedging herself between the orange crates, she tried to swallow the tight place in her throat. Tears seeped out, pushed by the pounding in her forehead. *No money. No home. No one. Gone.* Suddenly, Jo was afraid.

* * * * *

Jo stood in the red dirt road beside the tracks and watched the train grumble slowly away for a long few minutes. Her stomach echoed the deep hollow noise of the train. Her shoulders sagged heavily. *Church bells.* Jo turned toward the sound. People streamed from the wide open doors of a square white church. *A lot like our church, Father's church.* The men shook hands or thumped one another on the back, laughing. Children chased each other across the church yard, their Sunday clothes becoming untucked and dirt-smudged, or they tugged at their mothers' skirts, waiting for time to go home to the pot roast and fried chicken and steaming bowls of peas and mustard greens, the rice and light brown biscuits of Sunday dinner. Jo blinked and shook her head, mesmerized. Her stomach growled. She shrugged her pack over her shoulder again.

The town was larger than her hometown, and Jo wandered up the main street, past the post office and city hall, away from the tracks. In a store window, she found herself staring back: eyes vacant, gray face streaked where tears had washed through the dirt. It was a clown's face, neither boy nor girl. She didn't care. She pulled a piece of hay from her hair. She wondered where she was . . . who she was. *And where am I going? Who will I be?*

A train whistle called back down the hill, and Jo's head cocked toward it. She was more tired than she could remember, worn down to something empty and nameless. Her reflection was translucent, a ghost. Her

feet didn't seem able to follow the sound her ear
keened to. Jo pressed her forehead against the cool
glass. Her eyes focused on white ... white satin, white
lace, a white pearl ... *A wedding dress in the
window.*

"You there!" Jo started up and moved
instinctively toward the tracks, trying to walk fast,
but not too fast, not looking up. "You there!" the
voice called again. "Boy! Stop!" Jo stopped, took a
breath and peered up.

A woman stood at the gate of the parsonage
across the street. Younger than Jo's mother, her hair
beauty-shop waved, her Sunday dress fashionable and
just barely below her knee, she beckoned. "Come
here, young man." Jo hesitated. "Come on now," she
repeated, impatient.

"Yes ma'am?" Jo stepped into the street, then
stopped.

The woman looked her up and down. Jo wondered
what she saw. "I reckon you'll do," she said, opening
the gate. "Come on now." Jo stood in the street,
confused. The woman put her hands on her hips, her
brow wrinkling. "You need work, don't you?" she
said. "Food?"

Jo's stomach chuckled. She nodded. "Yes ma'am."

"And you'll work on Sunday?"

Jo grinned. "Yes ma'am."

The woman turned and started back up her walk.
"Well, come on then," she said over her shoulder.
"You'll work for me today." Jo followed her, suddenly
less tired. "The one good thing about livin' so close
to the tracks," the woman said, climbing the steps to

her porch, "can always get someone to do work." She mumbled to herself, "Honestly don't know how a preacher's wife is 'sposed to get anything done on a Sunday. Land sakes. Dishes in the sink, children tracking in mud."

Jo took the scrub brush and bucket the woman handed her. *I hate women's work.* Her stomach growled again and she sighed, thinking, and then smiled a little. *A boy would do a lousy job.*

Maxine watched the old lady purse her mouth and examine the wet, gleaming floor. She nodded slowly. "Very good," she said. "Very good indeed." She slowly uncrossed her arms. "You are a fine worker, Max," she said, tucking a strand of gray hair back up into her bun.

Maxine stood back to let her pass into the kitchen and watched her scoop peas and greens and a generous helping of cornbread onto a plate. "I dare say my grandsons wouldn't work so hard," the woman said. "Down on your knees, scrubbin' like that. Umph." Maxine let herself out onto the back porch and took the proffered plate through the door. She settled onto the steps, and the woman stood inside the screen talking.

"Now, Max," she said. "Someone is worrying about you back in New York, I am sure of it." She tssked and shook her head. "I know I would worry about my boys if they had taken off like this."

Maxine smiled up at her. She swallowed and wiped the butter from her mouth with her sleeve.

"Yes ma'am. I'm on my way home now," she said. *Home.* The word tasted good, like the cornbread melting on her tongue. She grinned at the woman again. "Yeah, going home."

The map was a maze of lines and labels. The finger tracing it was smudged, an eyebrow of dirt under the ragged nail. It wandered, then hesitated. Was this river the state border? Was this a boundary crossed? The roads curved across the white paper, sure and true, but the rails were somewhere else, invisible lines in the spaces between. *I'm going to have to find my own way, I guess.*

Jo folded the map, carefully avoiding the wind from the open door of the boxcar, and put it back in the pack under her head. She loved the neat folding, the smooth oil-skin paper, the even lines; she liked to try to figure out her place, where she had been, what she might expect. She loved the way the countryside, the cities, filled in as she traveled — markers, names, three dimensions — *the white spaces inside.*

She figured she was somewhere north of Colombia, South Carolina, maybe even in North Carolina, but it was hard to tell. That border had no easy marker, no river or town, just a line through a white space on a map. *Never been this far from home before.* She watched the farms and pine trees of the countryside roll by outside. *Going.* Jo smiled, feeling her insides expand as she breathed the air of this new place. She leaned back, the muscles in her back and arms already stronger, no longer aching, and only a few weeks on the road. She guessed it didn't much matter exactly where she was just now, just somewhere between the ordinary roads.

Maxine ran harder. The freight was just pulling out of the yard, not really moving fast yet, but she knew it would soon pick up speed. She tried not to watch the rusty wheels on the silver rails. Too easy to slip and fall under there. She'd heard of hoboes who'd been cut in half. *Focus on the ladder rungs, the boxcar door.*

A hand appeared out of the dark square, and she reached up for it, grabbing at the ladder rung in the same motion. Maxine swung up, the hand hauling her into the car. Inside, twenty or so men laughed and applauded as she sat down hard on the wood floor.

"Young Max!" Bert cried. "Welcome home."

* * * * *

The ties measured Jo's pace so that the *squish squish* of her shoes was like that of a soggy solo army. Her boxcar had been pulled off to a siding early in the afternoon, and she had ignored the big white clouds billowing up, her feet itching to keep on, keep going. She was sorry now.

Rain poured down her drooping hat onto her shoulders. Her clothes were drenched through. Her pants sagged, heavy with water, and she had to pull them up every few steps. The rails on either side of her gleamed, stretching ahead into the gray downpour.

No Joan of Arc in these shoes now. The rain was steady, not so hard as it had been for a while, and Jo smiled at the sound. When she had been younger, she'd run away to Jack's treehouse in a rainstorm, lain on the warm plywood floor and listened to the drum of rain on the tin roof, watched the leaves' slick dancing. Father had beat her while Mama cried. "You might have been killed, struck by lightning," she'd sobbed. Father's face had been tight, his mouth thin. "The Lord spares fools and children," he'd said, pulling the thin leather snake of his belt from the loops. "Twelve now," he'd said. "Hardly a child."

But it had been worth it, that sound of things of the sky and things of the earth meeting, washing together, blurring into something not quite earth, not quite sky. Jo stopped to hitch up her trousers and listened to the rain spattering into the mud. She smiled, wiping the wetness from her face.

Another sound. Jo glanced back over her shoulder, looking for the light of a train. Nothing. She heard it again. *Voices.* She scanned the trees. *There.* A light flickered through the woods and she heard another burst of laughter. Jo hesitated, but a flash of white split down the clouds into the woods ahead, and she jumped as the thunder cracked almost immediately. That was close. The rails gleamed wet on either side of her. *Iron. Steel.* Jo hitched up her pants and started down the embankment toward the light.

She found a path immediately and followed it to a clearing. Tin cans and trash littered the ground. A tar-paper-and-tin shack stood in the middle, smoke coming from its chimney, a lantern light flickering in the window. Men's voices. Jo took a step forward.

The door slammed open and Jo started back. "Gotta take a piss!" slurred the man staggering out. He saw Jo and stopped. "Who the hell are you?"

The doorway suddenly filled with ragged men, crowding to look out. *That boy . . . the one with the blue eyes . . .* Then Jo saw Bert.

"You!" She pointed at him. "That man's a thief!"

The other men burst into loud laughter.

"Sonny boy, which one do you mean?" guffawed one man.

A train whistle blew, off to the south, and Jo's head tilted toward it. She took a step back. *My money . . .*

Bert's eyes held hers. "Regular den a thieves you got here, Joe," he said slowly. He grinned, and his bad tooth became a dark hole in his mouth. He took a step forward, his eyes narrow. "But Joe's not your real name, is it, sonny boy?" Jo took a step back, her stomach clinching. Bert hissed, "You an' me's got a real sweet secret, huh?" She could smell the liquor on his breath. The other men stood in a semi-circle close behind Bert. The blue-eyed boy was gone. Jo wondered, quickly, if she had imagined him. "Bet all

47

these fellas 'd be mighty happy to know that sweet little secret, Joe." Bert blinked.

Jo turned and crashed back through the woods. A train rumbled just above. Wet leaves slapped at her face. Bert's laughter, low, was right behind her. She grabbed the trunk of a tree, pulled herself up the hill. She heard her breath: *ah, ah, ah.* Breaking twigs followed her. Jo forced her thighs to push upward, her toes digging into the mud. Slipping. Muck oozing between her fingers. She threw herself over the top of the embankment and scrambled to her feet, running before she was even upright.

Feet pounded just behind her. The hot, steamy breath of the freight pushed out into her face; the growl-squeal of iron wheels hurt her ears. She hardly noticed the rain. Jo scanned the boxcars as she picked up her speed, almost keeping pace with the train. The black square of a wide-open door. She pushed harder, lunged for it. Her hand closed around the cool, slippery rung. Eyes closed, Jo willed her burning shoulders to lift her up, and she swung into the car, rolling onto the wood floor.

She lay on her back, panting. The clack of the tracks underneath seemed loud, hollow, echoing in the empty car. A thud on the wall. Bert's gap-toothed black grin appeared in the boxcar doorway.

Jo caught her breath in a gasp. *Dang.* She glanced quickly around the car for a weapon. *Nothing.* Bert chuckled low as he pulled himself inside. "Sweet little secret," he hissed, moving toward her in a crouch.

Jo feinted toward the door, but Bert was not as

drunk as she thought. He lunged, and they both thudded to the floor.

"Sweet Jo," he grunted, grabbing her wrists, shoving his knee into her back. "Little bitch." Pinned. Jo struggled, gasping, but Bert's hands were tight, pinching hard. She felt her throat closing. *I will not cry.* He moved her hands to her sides and knelt on them, crushing her hands. He stank. Jo moaned. "I like secrets," Bert whispered, fumbling for her neck. Jo's forehead pounded with the clacks of the freight train over the tracks. She blinked hard, swallowed.

A thwack. "Uhhn." Bert fell forward onto her back, limp and heavy.

Off. Get him off! Jo wriggled free of the man and scrambled to the wall of the boxcar where she sat, panting. The blue-eyed boy stood looking down at Bert, a tree limb in his hand.

"Damn," he said. "I think I killed him." He knelt down and touched the blood on the back of Bert's head. He tried to shove the lifeless body over, but it was clearly too heavy. The boy looked up. "Think you could give me a hand with this?" The eyes were kind. Even in the dim light of the car, Jo could see the faint blue gaze, the reddish tint of the boy's hair. His overalls were baggy. He was not very big, not very tall . . . *ordinary*. He frowned. "Okay?"

"Uh, yeah," Jo said, glad for the dark, looking down to hide the blush she knew had crept up her neck. She knelt and helped him roll Bert over, trying not to shudder as she touched the warm body. "Um, thanks," she said, glancing up quickly.

The boy grinned. "You're welcome."

Maxine looked down at the boy. He was about her age, she guessed, thinner, taller. She couldn't see the green eyes and long dark lashes, but she knew this was the one she had reached out her hand to at that trestle bridge a week or so ago. *Guess he made a train after all.* She felt the tingle in the fingers he had touched, and warmth flooded her cheeks. Maxine was glad it was dark in the boxcar.

The tracks clacked a regular rhythm underneath their silence.

"You really think you killed him?" the boy said finally. His dark mop of hair gleamed in the dim light.

Maxine shrugged. "Don' know," she said. *Sure as hell wanted to.* She bent over Bert. "Maybe."

The boy took a deep breath and reached tentatively toward the body. Maxine saw that his hands were long, the fingers narrow, and they were shaking. "Son of a gun's got my money, I bet," he said.

Maxine squatted down. "Yeah?"

The boy glanced at her and squared his shoulders. "Yeah," he said, reaching into Bert's pockets one after another. "Robbed me a few days ago." He pulled a Buck knife from the last pocket and held it in his palm, looking at it. "Shoot." He put the knife on the floor and rested his hands on his knees. "Nothing."

Maxine watched the boy sit back on his heels,

biting his lip. "You ain't been around much, have ya?" she asked.

The boy's face got stiff, his jawline hard as he straightened up a little. "I've been around enough."

Maxine laughed. "Yeah, sure." She pulled Bert's leg over. "Look," she said, " 'Boes ain't gonna carry nothin' where it's easy ta get to." She nodded toward the knife. " 'Cept somethin' useful like that." Bert's shoe thumped down. Maxine untied the lace. "If you was carryin' cash in your pocket," she glanced up at the boy, "ain't no wonder ya got it robbed."

The boy was already working on Bert's other shoe. "I'm not . . . *ain't* that stupid," he muttered.

Maxine grinned. "No, I didn't think so," she said. She pulled off Bert's shoe. "Nope, not here." She watched the boy's fingers work. "How much did he get?" she asked.

He didn't answer.

"Ah." Maxine laughed. "Learned a lesson, huh. Bet he got ya ta take a drink outta that special bottle 'a his . . ."

The shoe finally off, the boy peeled some sweaty wet bills from the bottom of Bert's foot. "Yech." He counted the money and sighed. "Mostly gone," he said. He sat back again, his knees sprawling wide.

Maxine nodded. "Yeah, I kinda thought so," she said. "He's been spendin' pretty big on his buddies the last couple a days."

The look was long and speculative. "And you'd be one of his buddies?"

She gave a nod toward Bert. "Yeah, sure," she said. "I whack all my buddies over the head." The boy smiled. *Nice.* "Nah, I don't belong with nobody." *Nowhere.* "I just keep runnin' into him," she said, nodding to Bert. "Like lots of the guys out here." Maxine shook her head, thinking about all the folks she'd run into, over and over, looking for work, looking for something to eat, something to do, looking for their old life. *A new life.* "Lots of folks out here," she said.

"So I've been finding out," the boy said.

Bert groaned suddenly, and they both jumped back from him.

"Guess he's not dead," Maxine said, and they grinned at each other.

"Guess not," the boy said, and they both laughed.

"What the hell?" The railroad agent pointed to the side of the boxcar. His partner looked at the writing and shrugged. Someone groaned inside. The boxcar door slid stiffly, warped a little in the night's rain, and the agent had to lean into it to get it open. Inside, a hobo blinked at the light streaming in. He twisted, his wrists and ankles tied tight, and opened his mouth to reveal a gaping black tooth. "Look," said the agent to his partner. "If it's not the queen herself."

They dragged the hobo out and stood him upright to cut the ropes so he could walk. He blinked at the side of the train, dazed, maybe from the gash on the back of his head, maybe from the words, the chalk arrow, printed on the boxcar door: *Tea Party Here.*

* * * * *

Maxine pointed to the chalked *X* on the wall of the house. "Food here," she said to Joe. " 'Boes mark the places where you can get food." She led him around the side to the back door. "Now, we gotta give 'em a good story," she said, knocking. "Everybody likes to hear 'bout someone's worse off than they are."

The fire breathed in the night air, hissed in the mist and the damp hidden in the center of logs, and exhaled sparks, wisps of smoke, into the sky, to blur into stars, disperse into mist again.

"Stepfather, huh?" said Joe, his words as slow as something molten, somewhere between liquid and solid. "Sometimes I wish my father *was* dead."

Maxine wriggled the knife free, held the blade between her fingers and flipped it again into the log. It thunked, standing upright. The blade glowed orange, reflecting the flames of the campfire, and she saw her mother's tired face and sagging shoulders. *Wonder if he's been hitting her again.* She blinked and reached to pull Bert's knife from the log again.

"I guess my father was right about the liquor though," Joe said. Maxine glanced over and watched the long narrow fingers put the cigarette to his mouth, watched the lips close around the butt and draw in. Joe exhaled and the smoke curled around over his shoulder, fading up into the night sky. *He has such long eyelashes for a boy.* "It sure felt like that bottle had the devil's hand in it," he said, grinning over at Maxine.

She dropped her eyes, her neck burning, and slid her fingers along the silver blade. She hitched her shoulder back, trying to ease the pinch under her arm. *Damned binding.*

"Oh, I don't know," Maxine said, looking up again. "It's okay sometimes, the way it makes everything blur away." The blade warmed under her fingers. "You just got to be careful, take it slow, stay where you are, know who you are." She thought of her stepfather. "What it makes you." Joe watched the fire. "Makes some folks act mean," Maxine said, pinching the blade tighter.

Joe laughed. "Just made me sleepy," he said.

"Yeah." Maxine met his eyes. "But don't let Bert's stuff scare ya. It's got somethin' special in it."

The fire crackled, a log thunking as it rolled off. Joe grabbed a stick and pushed it back into the flames, squinting as he got close to the heat. "Prohibition, anyway," he said.

Maxine laughed. "That don't stop much of nobody. My stepfather's drunk 'most every night . . ." The knife twisted through the air and dug deep into the wood. From the corner of her eye, Maxine saw Joe start at the sound, his hard look at her. "There's gin joints all over in the city," she said, her voice a bit loud. She coughed and reached for the knife. "Harlem, the Village . . ."

"You mean in New York?" Joe said, his voice cracking. Maxine smiled.

"Sure," she said. "I told you I was from New York." His face was smooth, ruddy in the firelight, his eyes wide.

"What's it like?" His voice was hushed, the fire hissing behind it.

Maxine watched the fire, her eyes settling into a cubbyhole between sticks where the light wavered orange-white, almost like water. Her mind nestled into it like a warm room. "Aw," she said slowly, "the city's not all it's cracked up to be."

"It's got to be better than home," Joe said.

The crowded apartment, crowded streets, the dirt, noise, gray shadows, granite . . . *home.* Maxine bit her lip and looked down, away from the soft comfort of the fire. *Home. Do I still belong there?* She folded the knife blade in and it snapped shut.

"When I cross the Mason-Dixon Line, I'm never going south again." He looked up at the sky. "It doesn't feel like home anymore."

Maxine picked up a heavy stick and tossed it into the fire. *Home.* The sparks rained up into the sky and crossed some invisible line where they became stars.

It was good to travel with someone. Jo glanced over at Max. He'd taught her a lot about 'boing already. And he liked to talk too, didn't act annoyed at all her questions. *Never met a fellow like that before.*

"Damn it's hot," Max said. His boots scuffed at the rocks between the ties, and he took off his cap and wiped the sweat from his head.

"Yeah," Jo nodded, measuring her steps. Her shirt was soaked through, and she lifted her pack up to cool her back as she walked. "Another good reason to be going up North."

Max laughed. "Oh, it gets hot enough up there, you bet," he said. "You'll see."

Jo looked up, stretched, and wiped the sweat from her forehead. The twin rails wavered, merged into one and disappeared into the distant sky. Rows of tobacco plants stretched away from the rail bed, the lines of dark earth narrowing together, merging. Small figures, pickers, stood in the green as if at sea, far away. Jo wondered if this North Carolina county was their home, or if they were wanderers, workers traveling, like Max, from somewhere else, somewhere north.

"Does it snow a lot up there?" Jo asked, trying to imagine the storybook world, the white cold. "I've never seen snow."

"No?" Max stopped in his tracks and stared at her, his eyes wide, astounded, the blue edged with black bright against the hazy sky. "Never seen snow," he repeated in a low, wondering voice. "Whew." He looked over at her and grinned. "I mean yeah. Plenty a snow. And cold. Damn, it's colder 'n a —" He stopped and bit his tongue. "Well, plenty cold." He grinned. "You'll see."

"What's it look like?" Jo asked. "I mean, I read books and I saw some pictures, but what's it like?"

57

Max frowned. "Well," he said. "It's like, uh, really white. I mean, when it's comin' down heavy, a storm or somethin', it's like you can't tell where the sky ends and the ground starts, gray, except you're walkin' through it, and you kinda know in your head that you're walkin' on the ground, but it's hittin' ya in the face, all wet and white and soft and cold, and ya forget that there's anybody else, or maybe just who or what ya are, like ya get lost. And quiet, so quiet ya lose yourself and where ya are. And you have to watch for stuff, like street signs and stoops that you know . . ."

Jo watched Max, staring at the tracks, walking in rhythm with his words. *Not like any boy she'd ever known.*

"And it's like you're all alone maybe, in the white, in the world, or maybe you're just something else, something blank, or dark. And then when people come out of the snow, they'll almost walk right into you, cuz they don't see you either. And you can't tell who's who, or what they look like, just shape, size . . . all covered in white with the snow stuck all over." He stopped. "It's like most everything's blank," he said again. "Like you're starting from nothing." Max looked up from the tracks and grinned at Jo. "Inside, it's all cozy and warm, and that's where I'd rather be. But that's what it's like."

She smiled and looked down. He sure was different.

"I think I'd like to be in it," Jo said slowly. "Where everything is new, changed." *Where you can be anybody.*

Max laughed. "I'll wait for you inside."

58

Jo cocked her head. "I hear voices." She stopped to listen. Laughter drifted from up ahead somewhere. Max balanced on a rail and strained up on his toes. His overalls widened at the hips as he stretched. He's got a funny shape, Jo thought. "I think there's a bridge coming up," he said. They walked on, sweating, the rocks clacking and crunching, toward the sounds, the laughter soon punctuated with the splashing of water.

Jo felt her stomach caving in slowly. She knew what was up there. *Boys at a swimming hole.* Her insides became a little lighter, and the sweat suddenly felt cool on her forehead.

They stopped on the trestle bridge and looked down. A man swung out from the river bank far below on a rope, let go and splashed into the water. He was naked. About a dozen men and boys were in the water or scrambling up to take a turn on the rope swing, hair plastered down, laughing, and cool. A dark-haired fellow looked up and saw them. He waved, the line of black hair down his white belly stretching up as he raised his arm.

Jo quickly looked down at the black ties, her scuffed shoes. She'd seen naked boys at a swimming hole before. Heck, she'd swum *with* them ... till Mother found out. That talk on the edge of her bed. "Boys and girls are different," she'd carefully said. *I hadn't much noticed till then.* Jo felt her neck burn in the sun and silence. She glanced sidelong at Max. He was gazing off down the tracks.

"Um, water looks good, huh?" Max said to the sky.

Jo swallowed. "Uh, well ..."

Max scanned the horizon speculatively. He kicked the rail and put his hands in the back pockets of his overalls. A loud water-slap and splash below, followed by a shout of baritone laughter. Jo swallowed again. "Uh . . ."

"Don't really know if I'm in the mood for a swim," Max said suddenly. His voice seemed a little loud.

"Me either," she said quickly. "It's not that hot."

The man in the water shouted up, "Come on down, fellas! It's grand!" Jo looked over at Max, who met his eyes and blinked. His face seemed a little pale in the shadow of his cap. *What was that look?* A train whistle blew behind them, and Jo saw Max release a breath just as she felt her own stomach calm.

"I'm going to catch this train," she said hurriedly, already stepping across the bridge ties. She looked back at Max. "You can stay and swim if you want, but I haven't got time to waste. Gotta keep goin' north."

He was already following, and Jo felt something else inside catch and her checks flush warm.

"Oh, well," Max said, "if ya don't mind, I'll keep taggin' along with ya." They reached the other side of the trestle and stepped off the tracks to wait for the train. "Not sure whether I'm really goin' home, or if they'll want me back when I get there," he said, "but it's nice t'have a travelin' partner for a while."

Jo glanced at him and they both grinned. She shrugged, and they both looked off toward the whistle. "Yeah," Jo said, "sure. Probably need somebody to keep an eye on me anyway," she said.

Max flashed her a quick smile. "Never know when tea time'll catch up to you."

The top of the boxcar looked mostly flat, and the freight was moving slow, so Maxine scrambled up the ladder rungs, then waved Joe up behind her. "It's cooler up here," she called down over the roar of the wind. Maxine stretched out on her back and watched as pink begin to fringe the clouds overhead.

"This is wonderful," Joe shouted. Maxine looked over at him. The short fringe of his hair flew back in the wind, and she followed the freckled, high cheekbones down his smooth jaw, his pale neck.

"Lots better'n any ol' mud hole," Maxine yelled. She closed her eyes so she wouldn't look at him anymore. He thinks I'm a boy, she reminded herself. *Safer to keep it that way.* She felt the scuff of Joe's shoes on the wood as he moved closer, the warmth of his body. Maxine kept her eyes closed until he poked her.

"You gonna go home?" he asked. Maxine looked up to find the sharp, freckled angles of his cheeks and jaw close, the dark-lashed green eyes, staring down no more than a foot away. Joe sat cross-legged, hugging his knees, chin on his arms, his toe touching her arm. Maxine sat up, and his face reddened. "Sorry," he said. "I don't like to yell." *Was that a blush?*

Maxine shrugged. "It's okay. You just surprised me." They watched the sun lowering over the trees, the low hills in the west. Clouds changed color, streaked with pink, orange, purple, shifting their costumes for evening, for some other life at night. "I don't know where I'm going." Maxine rested her chin on her hands and thought of her mother, the kids, her stepfather and his fists. "Don't much want to go home," she said. "Not while *he's* still there."

"Your stepfather?" Joe asked. "Why?" His voice was a medium-soft tone. Maxine liked the way he always pronounced his words so neat, the warm accent behind them.

She hesitated. "He just ain't ... isn't real nice," she finally said. "Hits my mother, the kids. Drinks." The words caught. Maxine blinked and looked down, swallowing. "He said I was bad. No good." She glanced at Joe, who was listening, watching her. She looked down again. "He said I didn't belong there." She bit her lip. "My mama gave me all her money. Said to go up to Lowell to the mills. Got a cousin up there 'sposed to get me work. He's a butcher." Maxine thought of Cousin Nat, the way he had looked at her, and she shivered. "Aw," she muttered, shrugging, "I didn't want to spend my life in no mill, no shop ... And there wasn't no work anyway. Bosses all say m ... folks with fam'lies need the work more." She grinned shyly up at Joe. " 'Sides, I wanted to see something of the world before ..." She bit her tongue. *Before I get married.* "Well, just wanted to see the rest of the world," she finished hurriedly.

Joe laughed. "So you saw the South?" He crowed.

Maxine jabbed him in the arm. "Hey, first train was goin' that way." She laughed.

Joe picked up a pine cone from a crevice, and Maxine first flinched, then snatched it out of the air as he threw it, the wind slowing its force. A gunshot cracked and the wooden roof splintered to her left. They both jerked around to look.

A railway agent stood on the boxcar behind them, his gun leveled at them. "Hands up, boys!" he shouted. "Free ride's over!" He was young, with splotches on his face, and Maxine could see that his hands were shaking. Maxine met Joe's eyes, then looked slowly down at the ladder rungs under him, and then back into his eyes. Joe's body blocked hers from the agent's view, and she could see the uniform and wavering pistol advancing slowly over the roof of the car. She led Joe's eyes down and opened her hand to show him the pine cone there. He looked up again and nodded. Joe crouched to his feet and Maxine began to stand up.

"Nice and easy now!" the agent shouted, his voice cracking. "Get those hands up!"

Maxine whipped the pine cone in a hard fast ball, just like she had learned in the alley at home, right at the agent's spotted face. His hands flew up and he wobbled. She dropped to the ladder rungs, scrambling down, almost in Joe's arms, his breath on her back. "Hey, hold it, you bums!" the agent shouted, and Maxine heard his feet as he jumped to their boxcar.

Joe was suddenly gone. Maxine glanced back and saw him in the dimming light, rolling away down a grassy hill. The smells of hay, animals, earth rushed around the train. She saw her shoes on the last rung. *Gotta jump.* The black ties flashed by under her feet, blurring, and the gap over the rocky rail bed to the soft grass seemed impossibly wide.

"Hey!" She looked up to see the agent looking down from the roof. "Stop!" His voice broke. Maxine glanced over her shoulder.

"Come on!" called Joe's voice from the darkness. "Jump!" Something in Maxine's chest grabbed at the sound, already fading, and she swallowed her heart, forced her thigh muscles to bunch tighter, and flung herself out into the sweet-smelling grayness.

Jo didn't know how much longer she could carry Max. She thought she saw a flickering in the darkness ahead, but it appeared and disappeared like some kind of trickster's magic. He wasn't very heavy, but Max kept losing consciousness, sagging down against her side, his toes dragging in the dirt of the road. She smelled food. She boosted him higher again, gripping his sweaty wrist tighter and holding his waist — *narrow, and something thick under his shirt* — in the circle of her arm.

He'd been out for a good ten minutes after he fell from the train. His face had been pale, and the blood from the gash on his head streamed down his neck. When his eyes finally fluttered open, Jo sniffed back her tears quick, and she didn't think he noticed in the dark. *Boys don't cry.*

"Ankle hurts," he said. She splinted it up, solid, with some branches and the ribbon that had held her lock of hair. Max lay still, his eyes closed, and when she finally tried to get him upright, he nearly passed out again, swaying against her shoulder, trying hard to prop himself up with the limb she'd cut for a cane. Jo had nearly carried him for the last mile or two, and her legs and backed ached.

"Here! You kids, come on and eat now!" A woman's voice shouted out into the night. "Janie! Billy! Come here right now! Time you was gettin' to bed soon now."

There was a mishmash of rusted automobiles, tin and wooden shacks, canvas tents and tattered quilts, bedrolls on the ground. *A hobo jungle.* It wasn't home, but it was a good place to rest. Children's laughter, then two small shadows passed through a campfire light. More lights, lanterns, were scattered around. Voices mumbled in the dark. She dragged Max forward.

"Look, Mama!" a child said.

"Why whatya know," came a deeper voice from the other side of the road. Jo stopped in the middle of a dirt crossroad and looked down each of the dark lanes, confused. Figures appeared from the shadows, stepped into the lights of the fires.

"Who's that, Mama?" said the child.

The woman standing at the fire looked up. "Now what." She started toward Jo and Max. "Janie, get me the blanket from the tent." Jo let Max slide down, and she sank to her knees beside him, holding his head with its thick red-orange hair. A crowd of people encircled them, their faces lined and their eyes soft. One fellow — *a woman?* — stood with her feet wide apart, dressed in men's pants and jacket, hands on hips, a little apart from the crowd, and a woman with silky black hair pressed close, gripped his . . . *her* arm. Jo stared at them for a long second. *Both women? The big one must be a man.* An old fellow scratched his unshaven whiskers and shook his head, kneeling down. Jo looked at the woman from the cook pot who pushed forward. "I think he's broken his leg, ma'am," she said.

She saw the woman in trousers exchange a glance with her friend. "It's okay," said the first woman, touching the blood on Max's head, the splint on his leg. She smiled kindly at Jo and touched her arm. "Don't worry, hon. Think of the jungle as home."

" 'Course they're both women," Max said. Jo stood behind him, lifting up locks of his hair, slicing through them with scissors borrowed from Lizzie, the woman who had helped them that first night in the Hooverville, the hobo jungle. Max shifted his leg, propped on a wooden crate, wrapped fat with make-shift bandages. Lucky it wasn't broken. "Not too short," Max said again. "I don't like my hair short." His voice was tense.

Jo looked at the tent across the dirt road that belonged to Sam and Wit. *Two women.* Jo watched her fingers divide out a section of hair, silky between her fingers. She tried to cut off about as much as the other parts, just a little.

"You really think they're both women?" she said

finally. Jo wanted to ask why, what did it mean? but all the right words seemed stupid . . . *gray.*

"I know so," Max said. "Look, there are joints back in New York, in the Village and up in Harlem too, where there were lots of women like that, and men too, fellows dressed up like girls even, I heard."

Jo concentrated on cutting the hair. *Why?* "Dang," she said. "My father said New York was the devil's workshop." She felt her chin stiffening like his.

"Aw, ain't nothin' all that bad in it, I reckon," Max said. "Just folks play-actin' . . . like in the theaters 'n stuff."

Jo glanced up just in time to see Sam and Wit emerge from the tent. They grinned and waved. Sam tipped her hat. "Howdy, boys!" She drew out the second word, mockingly. *She knows I'm a girl.* Jo swallowed hard.

"Something wrong in it," she muttered.

Sam glanced at them again and then pulled Wit into a hug, both of them smiling. She tilted the smaller woman's chin up with her hand and looked into her eyes. Jo felt her mouth dropping as she watched Sam lower her mouth to Wit's, the smaller woman's body curving in, leaning up into Sam's lips. *Only boys are supposed to kiss girls like that.* They pulled apart, and Sam looked back over and winked.

Jo dropped her eyes to the top of Max's head and tried to ignore the blush warming her cheeks. She grabbed another lock of hair and snipped. Max cleared his throat and his head bobbed down. Neither of them watched Wit and Sam, but Jo heard their footsteps crunch off in the gravel. *I'm not like that.*

Something crinkled at the back of her neck, a sound like the onion-skin edge of her map.

The scissors opening and closing seemed comforting, loud, clean, and smooth. A cardinal peeped at the edge of the woods. Children played farther down the road, and someone — maybe Lizzie — was cooking something that smelled earthy, like potatoes. Jo and Max both kept silent.

The camp was lively, folks coming and going all the time. Mostly, they all threw in whatever they had, and the pot was full. Richmond was less than ten miles away and during the day, some of the folks would go in and beg or look for odd jobs or maybe lift a can of beans from the store. Some of them, like Lizzie and her kids, lived in their old automobile, looking for enough money to buy more gas, get farther down the road. "Husband's gone," she'd said. "Lookin' for work down the rails. Just left one night." She'd been waiting for him to come back for a month. And every day, new men passed through the camp, and Jo knew someone was waiting somewhere for each of them to come back. But probably not for me, she thought. *Probably glad I'm gone.*

"So, I guess it was lucky your leg wasn't broken, huh?" she said, looking carefully around the edges of Max's hair for uneven patches, trying not to think about the way Sam had kissed Wit. Maybe Sam's not a girl, she thought, but she knew what she had seen.

"Yeah, I 'spose," Max said. He hesitated, and Jo could see his hands open and close in his lap below. "You know..." He swallowed, then took a breath. "You don't have to wait around for me if you don't want." His hands opened and closed. Jo felt her fingers stiffen around the metal handles of the scissors. "I mean, you havin' to get up North to go to college and find that lady and all . . ." Max's shoulders seemed to sag a little.

Jo stopped cutting and stood looking down at the beautiful deep red of Max's head. She swallowed. "Um, well, you need some help with that foot," she began. The words began to come faster. "It's gonna be sore for a long time and well, I kinda figure I owe you now . . . your saving my life and all. Twice now." She took a breath. "It's only the end of July," she said. "I've got till September."

Max's shoulders seemed to relax. He twisted to look back up at Jo. "Reckon I'm not much use on my own just now." He grinned.

"Besides," Joe said, "I kind of like pallin' around with you."

Maxine watched a lock of her hair twirling down to the dirt. Joe's hands on her head were warm, solid. *Holding me.* "It kind of reminds me of me and my brother," Joe said. "Different, but —"

"Yeah," Maxine murmured, lulled by the fingers in her hair, the quiet snip-snip of the scissors. "Like fam'ly."

Jo stood, her mouth wide, in the doorway of the cathedral. It was huge. Max's footsteps echoed up the aisle, an uneven tempo as he limped. The sprain was nearly healed, and they'd come into town looking for a day's work or some food to contribute to Lizzie's pot.

"We were always together in church," Max said. "My mama made sure of that, until Mick —" He stopped and glanced back at Jo. "My stepfather. He said something to Father Casey, and then we couldn't go back anymore. So I used to sneak around and go to other churches."

Jo watched as Max knelt at the altar and crossed himself, his lips moving. Looking up at the stained glass windows, he said softly, "I missed the part about bein' part of God's fam'ly . . . All one fam'ly."

"It's plenty big," Jo said, walking forward, trying to be quiet. The church was like something out of a picture book, foreign. The smooth stone walls swept up into a peaked ceiling, the tall windows letting in an eerie, calming light. *Father's little church would fit three times inside here.* Dust motes shimmered up through stream after stream of light, whole universes swirling through space.

"Aw, this is nothing compared to St. Patrick's," Max said. Jo watched him walk to a row of tall wooden boxes on the side of the church. He touched one lightly with his fingertips.

"May I be of service to you two young men?"

"Ah!" Jo felt her skin jump and she let out a little cry. The nun was standing right behind her. She'd never even seen a real nun before.

The woman's face, small and round — *everything else about her hidden inside those black robes* — was kind. She smiled and Jo felt her own shy smile well up.

"Thank you, sister," Max said behind her. "I just wanted to . . ." He faltered.

The nun waited a second, Max's words fading away, then said, "Are you boys hungry?"

Jo looked back at Max, his eyes, the blue ringed in black, meeting her glance, holding a second. She blinked. "Yes, sister," Max said, still staring. The nun turned and Max followed her. Jo stood for a while, watching the dust motes glittering up and around the vast air, whole other places, worlds different and worlds the same.

The line was ragged, shifting and sagging as the people in it changed course, turning to speak to others, or slumping as if to disappear into themselves.

"He were a bank pres'dent," someone murmured, his thumb poking the air toward a small man, made smaller by his blank eyes, his chin resting on his chest, no shirt under his filthy gray suit. Two children pushed and shoved each other, giggling, the pot between them clunking the shins of others, the line a game for them.

"Lotta good that march done in June... Washin'ton, shit," came another voice. A baby cried and fussed.

"Got my ear cut off over there in that riot by the

Potomac." A barefoot woman in a yellowed hat with drooping feathers leaned heavily against the jamb as she reached the door.

"Jungle . . . Hooverville outside of town, west," someone said.

"Hear there's work in Detroit," someone else murmured.

Bert was part of the line, mean and distant, his own angry link. He scowled down at the floor, said nothing, shoving ahead when he could, listening to the fragmented conversations around him.

"Baby died in the boxcar comin' through the mountains," said a toneless voice. "In the tunnels. Dark. We was packed tight. Choked, I reckon." Someone laughed loud across the room. A woman in a threadbare but finely stitched dress held a lace hanky to her nose, clutched her purse to her chest and shuffled forward with the line. "Might be better off 'n any of us . . ."

"More potatoes, please," Maxine shouted. She wiped her steamy forehead on her sleeve, grabbed another bowl and spooned a potato from her pot into it. Joe's hand touched hers as she passed him the bowl and she met his eyes. He ducked his head and ladled broth over the potato. The next person in the soup line took the bowl from his hand.

Maxine felt a light touch on her shoulder and looked back. Sister Anne motioned to her and Joe, and two other workers stepped into their places. "Must be tea time," Joe said.

Jo took the plate from Sister Anne and sat at the long table watching Max. *He sure is different.* His face opened up, softened, as he talked to the nun. Jo liked the way his pale lashes seemed to fade away in the bright sunlight.

And Sister Anne ... *She's different too.* Her long habit nearly touched the stone floor. It hid all of her except her face, which was creased and dark with sun. *She could be anyone too.*

Maxine studied Joe's face as he concentrated on his hand, flat on the wooden box in front of him. Quiet, going-to-bed camp sounds seeped through the tar-paper walls and open doorway of the shack they had claimed while her sprained ankle was healing. Joe played slowly, carefully sticking Bert's knife into the orange-crate table. *He is beautiful.* Maxine smiled to herself and shook her head. *Handsome.* Frowning a little, Joe's eyes gleamed in the candlelight, bright green through the dark fringe of those long lashes. *Wasted on a boy.* Maxine liked the light hairs on his straight jaw and the pale freckles on his long nose. She'd never seen him shave. She wondered if he was as old as he said — sixteen, two years younger than her. He sure was different from other boys she'd known; sometimes he seemed lots older than sixteen. Sometimes he seemed different from every other boy she'd ever met. He bit his lip as she watched, faltering in his game.

"Go slow," Maxine said gently.

Joe sighed and stopped. He looked up. "I'm not very good at this."

Maxine grinned. "Maybe I should teach you poker instead."

Joe laughed and picked up the knife again. "If my father could see me now ..." He glanced over at Maxine, and she felt her chest tighten. She held her breath for a second, his eyes holding hers. *Does he see that I'm a girl?* Joe took a deep breath. "Let me try it one more time."

He spread the fingers of his left hand open and flat on the crate, and they both concentrated on the knife in his right. The tip touched the crate between the long pale fingers: *tap, tap, tap, tap, tap.* This time Joe didn't hesitate and the knife started backwards the way it had come: between the thumb and index finger, the index and middle ...

"Yow!" The knife clattered to the crate and Joe stuck his fourth finger in his mouth.

"Damn!" Maxine said, her stomach twisting. "Let me see." Joe placed his hand flat on hers. Maxine breathed in. Her palm tingled.

The cut was small, just barely bleeding. They both stared at the drop that welled up from it, curling over and around Joe's finger, suddenly warm and damp in Maxine's palm. Her fingers stroked up lightly against his palm. "Nothing ..." Joe's voice was soft, hoarse. "It's nothing."

He pulled his hand back and they both looked up. Maxine felt the blood in her hand, sticky. Joe didn't blink. His forehead held a narrow crease.

A crash outside. The night silence erupted. Screaming, shouts. Sounds of feet running. "Billy, grab the blankets!" came Lizzie's cry. Maxine and Joe both looked at the doorway. A light — fire. Shadows rushed by. Sam's face, pale, appeared.

"Main Streeters!" she gasped. "They're bustin' us up! Get out!" she shouted and disappeared into the dark.

Maxine jumped up, grabbing her bedding from the dirt floor. "Come on! Get your stuff!" Joe scrambled to his feet, his mouth open. "Come on," Maxine ordered. "They'll beat us up if they catch us." She reached down and grabbed the blanket from the ground where Joe had been sitting and stuffed it into his arms. "Run!"

Outside, people ran in every direction. Shadowy figures holding torches advanced down the road toward them, flames lighting the sky as the jungle burned behind them. Maxine saw someone grab the arm of a hobo and the shadow of his club as it smashed down. Lizzie, the two little ones at the ends of her hands, ran, dragging them along toward the woods. Joe stood, his mouth open and eyes wide, watching the men march closer. Maxine gave him a shove. "Run, Joe," she said, and he shook himself out of his trance and sprinted ahead. Maxine limped after him, her ankle jolting pain up her thigh every time she put her left foot down. Joe's long legs stretched out as he gathered speed, his shadow darkening. He glanced back and stopped dead.

Maxine waved him ahead. "Run!" she yelled. She looked over her shoulder. They were getting closer, some of the men breaking off from the pack as they grabbed stragglers and shoved torches into tents and shacks. She saw Wit kneeling, a man holding her arm, his fist smashing into her jaw. A shadow loomed up, dark against the firelight — Sam. Maxine caught her breath as the shadow raised up and smashed a board over the man's head. He crumpled to the ground.

"Come on!" Joe grabbed her around the waist, half-carrying her as they ran. "Like the three-legged race, remember?" His grin flashed white at her, and Maxine cocked her left knee and synchronized her right with Joe's pace over the empty field. A full moon dipped low behind the woods, the shadows of trees soft and welcoming against the white light.

Jo watched the back of Max's bowed head, the white of his bare neck, his hair glinting gold in the strange light of moon through stained glass windows. *He's kind of beautiful.* Jo blinked. *Handsome.* The dark altar where he knelt, the wooden pews where she sat, the stone floors — all were striped in mosaics of bright color and gray. Shadows fringed the silent, empty church. Max had made her come here. She shivered. They were alone. He crossed himself and began to stand up.

"I want to get out of here," Jo said. She closed her eyes. The vision flashed again into the bright lights behind her lids: the man's fist smashing into Wit's jaw, the way her head had snapped back, the way the man had crumpled to the ground when Sam's huge shadow had clubbed him. She felt sick.

Max walked toward her, his footsteps hollow, uneven and slow. "The nuns won't care," he said, shrugging. "It's safe here."

Jo sat down in a pew, put her feet on the seat

and wrapped her arms around her legs. "It doesn't *feel* safe." Her chin dropped to rest on her knees.

Max sat down at the far end of the same pew and propped his ankle on the back of the row ahead. They both stared into the empty church.

"Why?" Jo said, remembering Lizzie touching her arm as Max lay on the ground beside her that first night, Lizzie dropping whatever anyone had into her cook pot, feeding anyone who came along. Lizzie framed in firelight, her two children tugging at her skirts. *Where would she wait for her husband to come back to now?* "Why did those people do that?" she wondered aloud. "Who were they?"

Max sighed. "Main Streeters. Regular people. Citizens."

Jo thought about her father. "Signs of the last days," he'd said of the beggars who'd come to the door, the hard times. "Behold, the judge standeth at the door."

Max sighed again. "Makes 'em feel bad to see us, I reckon. Reminds 'em of what could happen to them, maybe."

Jo stared down at her hands, the patterned lights dancing on them. Her father's face, hard-lined and red, shouting from the pulpit throbbed a headache into her temples. "I don't much like churches," she said.

"It's safe here."

Jo pushed her thumbs into her temples. She looked over. Max was staring at her. "What if I don't want to stay?"

Max bit his lip and looked out into the church. "Then don't."

Jo didn't move. Her stomach felt empty, more than empty, hollow. She looked down at her hands again. From the edge of her vision, she saw Max pull out his blanket. He stretched out on the wooden pew toward her. Jo frowned. *I don't want to go.* Her fourth finger throbbed and she remembered the cut. The blood had dried. *I don't want to go without Max.* He turned over again, his shoes thumping the wood, then he sat up. Jo sucked on her finger. *Does he want me to go?* She felt like crying.

"Hey," Max scooted closer along the slick wooden seat. "I forgot. How's the finger?"

Jo smiled. "Okay," she said, holding it out. "Nothing." She felt warm on the side where Max sat. She glanced at him. "How's the foot?"

"Okay."

Their voices disappeared into the air in the high reaches of the church. Unmoving, they both stared out toward the altar, in the silence.

"So you gonna stay or go?" Max finally asked.

Jo swallowed, the colored shadows blurring. "You want me to stay?" The words drifted up and the echo faded to silence.

"Sure."

She glanced over at Max, who slowly turned his head to look at her. *His eyes are so blue.* Jo looked down at her lap quickly, her neck burning. "Okay," she said.

"Okay."

Jo stood up and opened her pack, fumbling the strings into a knot, her fingers uncontrollable. She bit her lip. Max stood and rearranged his blanket. Jo tried not to get too close. She pulled her blanket out and shook the dirt from it.

They sat down at the same time. Jo felt her shoulder touch his. His mouth opened, as if to say something, and then his pale orange lashes half lowered. Jo's heart thudded into her throat, and she leaned, her body pulled like a tide toward him. She felt his breath, warm on her upper lip. His mouth pressed into hers, and Jo heard an echo, as if her heartbeats were footsteps on the stone floor, and the lights behind her lids blurred into the mosaic of full moon through stained glass windows.

Max's hand was on her thigh. Jo's leg burned, trembling, the muscle tense. She placed her palm flat on his chest. *That thickness.* He flinched. Their tongues touched, shy, then something seemed to buzz somewhere inside.

They pulled back at the same instant. She saw them then as if from the pulpit . . . *two boys kissing.*

"I —"

"It's —" Jo started at the same instant. He paused, and she rushed on. "It's okay, I'm really a girl, Max." His face changed.

"My name isn't Jo, it's Josephine, but that's what they call me, Jo." Mac's skin had paled, but Jo couldn't stop the words that poured out from her. "I wanted to tell you before but I . . . so it's okay. I just —" Max's face had become whiter, and his body drew back a little. Jo stammered, "I just . . . well, you're different from the other boys I knew. I'm not like those other women that were dressed like men," she said. He was blinking fast now. "It's just my brother's clothes," she explained. "I can look like a girl too . . ." Jo heard the odd note in her voice. *I can look like a girl too.* She stopped, out of breath.

Max didn't speak.

"What's wrong?" Jo asked, her stomach falling in on itself.

"Uh, I uh . . ." He clamped his jaw shut and looked away into the darkness. His face had begun to redden. *He's mad.*

"I'm sorry," Jo said, trying not to cry. *Boys don't cry.* Her voice became smaller than it had been since she'd cut her hair. "I, well, I just liked you. I'm sorry, I thought you . . ." Something wet slipped down her cheek. She looked at her hands cradled limp in her lap. *Dumb, I feel like a dumb girl.* She tried to stiffen her jaw and glanced at him.

"You should have said something," Max said, the creases over his eyebrows shadowed, the blacks of his eyes full. "I mean sooner." He paused for a long time. "I . . ." Air came out of his lungs in a hot puff. "Damn."

Jo had stopped breathing. Max spoke to his lap. "Yeah," he said, angrily. "I like you fine." Her ears zinged. "Fine," he said and thunked his head on the back of the pew in front of him.

Max's face kept changing, lurching from one expression to another. He was blinking fast. *What is he thinking? Why doesn't he look at me?* Max swallowed again and again, the corners of his mouth pulling down. Something damp glinted in the corners of his eyes.

The door behind them thudded open with a wooden echo. "Who's here?" Sister Anne called.

"Me," Max croaked. "Just us."

Jo started to get up, gathering her pack.

"No, no," said Sister Anne, patting Jo on her shoulder. "Stay, stay." Lizzie and the children entered the church behind her. "I know what's happened," she said. "More will be coming soon. This place is for all God's children."

"You'll need help, Sister," Max said, jumping up and following her back out.

Jo started to follow him, but Janie grabbed her hand. The little girl pulled her down, and she watched Max's back, her chest hollow as he walked away.

"You've got to tell Billy," Janie said, whispering loudly. "Tell him it's okay for boys to cry."

The dawn was overcast, indefinite, gray. Breezes spattered the sidewalks, the streets, with drops from the leaves, and the early riser hunched, expecting another downpour. She . . . *he* scurried on. Nothing was clear. A fog of steamy trails, the scarves of a dancer, drifted, tattered, toward the river, but there was no sun, no sky really, just different shades of gray. *With no dawn, how do you know when it's a new day?*

Maxine stumbled as she stepped down off the curb, her hands deep in her pockets, and glanced back up the hill to Richmond's steeples and tall buildings. *Guess you just don't know. Guess you go on, wandering in the gray.*

The silver of rails, another gray, stretched, branching and curving like an elaborate, bare and perfect tree into the freight yard. Maxine walked quietly, peering through the mist for railway agents, looking for a boxcar, a train ready to leave. *North.* Maxine was going home. *Where I belong.*

The sky seemed a little lighter, or maybe it was just the air. She wondered if Joe — *Josephine* — she turned the name over in her head — was awake yet. *Wonder if she knows I'm gone.* Maxine stepped up, balancing on a silver-gray rail. *I'll miss him.* Without thinking, her fingers touched her lips. She blinked. *He . . . she wouldn't have done that if she'd known I was a girl. Why didn't I see it?* She shook her head sharply, mad again. The rail was slick with dew. She wavered, slipping, and held her arms out for balance. *Would I have kissed her if I had known?*

Jo struggled out of sleep. Something was wrong in her dream. Someone was changing . . . *going into gray.* She sat up on the hard pew, her back and shoulders stiff and aching. She couldn't remember the dream. She'd been afraid, and there was something else. Jo looked around, blinking in the bright, colored light.

"Max?" She heard the note, high — *like a girl* — in her voice. Gone. "Max!" Her voice echoed in the church, the fear and question mark dissolving into dust motes and air. She leaned forward until her forehead rested on the back of the pew in front of her. Palms up, her hands lay spread in her lap, and the lines in them blurred. *He must hate me.*

"Is everything all right, child?" The nun's voice

was soft, just behind her, and Jo heard her neck crack as she started up. She grabbed her blanket and stuffed it into her bag.

"Yes ma'am, I'm sorry, I'll get out, I mean . . ." Jo fumbled with the buckles on her pack.

Sister Anne's hand rested softly on her shoulder. "Don't worry, child." Her hand was warm and comforting. Jo closed her eyes and rubbed her forehead. "I saw your friend, Max, this morning," she said, softly so as not to wake the others.

At Max's name, Jo looked up, her heart thudding an extra beat. "You saw Max?"

"I imagine he's flipping a freight toward Washington by now, Joe," the nun said gently. "He said to tell you that he had decided it was time to go home now." She studied Jo's face.

Jo swallowed. "Do you know where?" she asked, her voice catching.

The nun shook her head. "No, no. New York City somewhere." She patted Jo's arm. "Now I've got to see to starting some breakfast." She turned, saying, "Another friend of yours is here today too."

"Huh?" Jo stood up. "Um, I mean, I'd help, ma'am, but, I mean, um, I think I've got to be headin' on myself now . . ." Itching, the soles of her feet were pointed toward the huge double doors, and she found herself alert to the sounds of the tracks.

"Why in such a hurry, young Joseph?" Jo's stomach pitched, then clenched, as she turned toward Bert's voice. He stepped from behind the confessionals carrying a broom. He grinned. "Got a date for tea?"

Jo shuddered, her ears humming, then she ran.

* * * * *

Maxine huddled in a corner of the boxcar, hugging her knees to her chest. A woman sat nearby, a toddler on her lap, her husband's arm around her shoulders. They were young, not much older than she. An ordinary family. *And what am I?* She thought of Cousin Nat and shivered. The man sang in a low quiet hum. There were maybe forty or fifty 'boes in this car, Maxine figured.

Slits of pale light seeped between the wooden boards of the wall. Rain drummed hard on the roof and the train groaned and rumbled as it rocked along. Maxine watched the steady drips of water jerk and splash with the movements of the train. The others clumped together in groups, away from the wet. It would be a long, slow ride to New York — lots of switches, Baltimore, Philly, lots of agents. And what would any of them find in the city, Maxine wondered. *What will I find?*

The child on the woman's lap looked out with large eyes, staring at Maxine. The mother's head drooped to her husband's shoulder, and he smiled to himself, the faint lines etched with grime smoothing from his forehead. Maxine shivered at a sudden draft through her jacket and around her neck. She bit her lip, and the baby smiled and gurgled at her, twisting in her mother's lap. Maxine dropped her head to her knees and closed her eyes.

"Makin' eyes at the girls, Max?" The voice was soft and musical, but it held also a note which was flat, almost dead.

Maxine looked up into Wit's kind brown eyes,

wisps of dark hair framing her face, so pale in the light that she seemed a ghost. Maxine felt herself smile.

Wit scrunched down into her corner, her knees and legs warm against Maxine's, close in the dry spot. She tucked her dress under her demurely, glancing at Maxine from under dark lashes. Like Joe's, Maxine thought. She scanned the car again. "Where's Sam?"

Wit frowned, her plucked-thin eyebrows arching inward. Maxine had a sudden vision of a man's arm, silhouetted against the flames, smashing a club downward, Sam crouched on the ground. Her stomach caved in. "Is he, uh, she okay?" Maxine heard her voice rise.

Wit reached out and smoothed her arm with cool fingers. "She's fine, Max." She let her fingers rest on Maxine's arm and smiled when she met her eyes. "They hauled her in after she busted one of them Main Streeters in the mouth. She got a pretty good bump on the head, but he looked worse, I can tell you." Wit shrugged. "Told me to wait for her back in New York is all." Wit's eye closed in a wink. "Thinks I'll be safer there."

The place on Maxine's arm where Wit's fingers still rested had begun to burn. She felt her face flush warm for no reason, and she dropped her eyes.

Wit laughed softly, with that same musical note. "You think you'll be safer in New York, Max?" she asked, drawing her name out in a long teasing question. *She sees me.*

Maxine coughed to clear her throat. "Goin' home," she mumbled.

"Ahhh," Wit said, sitting back and looking her up

and down, speculatively. Maxine met Wit's eyes. Wit nodded slowly in the long silence. She smiled, her eyes gentle, and reached out and ran her fingertips through Maxine's short hair. "And how will you explain this to Mama?"

Jo trotted slowly along the web of tracks leading out of town. The freights all sat idle, silent. A passenger train was loading and as she hurried past it watching for conductors and railway agents a woman looked down at her, frowning sadly through the glass window. Something about her eyes reminded Jo of her mother and she felt a short pang of homesickness. The engine puffed smoke and ash, a slow animal chained like a circus performer to its tracks. Jo jogged on through the black steamy cloud, north along the silver rails, hoping for an empty freight.

She glanced back as the train whistle screamed. Something moved, appearing behind her out of the steam cloud. *Bert. Dang.* He grinned and picked up his feet a little faster.

The passenger train huffed and the wheels slipped round then caught, and it jerked out of the station. Jo's heart thumped and her ears began to ring. She'd never hopped a passenger train. Bert was gaining on her. *Gonna have to do it.*

As the engine passed her, Jo veered closer. She saw the fireman, his muscles gleaming with sweat as he shoveled coal, but he didn't notice her jogging alongside. The train's speed was gaining. An iron rung ladder crept closer, and she grabbed it —

practiced, strong now — and swung herself up, her feet finding the bottom step easily. She looked back.

Three cars behind, Bert grinned at her. He was still loping along. Jo frowned, brushed off her clothes, climbed up to the platform and opened the door into the front of the car.

The long corridor between compartments was dim. Fourth class would be near the back of the train. Jo touched her shirt. *Maybe I have enough money left to pay the fare.* She started to reach into the binding, but the door at the far end opened. A young woman wearing a fashionable hat stared at her. Jo blushed. A shadow loomed behind the woman . . . *Bert.*

She didn't think, but reached for the nearest door handle and stepped into the compartment. *Empty!* The car rattled as the train picked up speed. The outskirts of Richmond flashed by the window. Jo smiled grimly, her lips tight and temples pounding. A black umbrella with a heavy gold handle lay on the velvet seat. *Time I took care of this myself.*

The narrow wooden door opened. "Tea time, young Jose . . ." It was Bert. Jo stood on the seat. She grimaced, then brought the gold knob of the umbrella handle down hard on his temple. He slumped and pitched forward into the compartment. Her stomach turned with the dull thud.

She dragged him inside, remembering that night Max had muttered those same words. "Tea time," she muttered grimly.

The river sleeps, wide and flat, a lazy moat, like a fat guard, drowsing with his feet on the desk, and the land it guards is not country, not state, but district, an arbitrary portion of place, imaginary lines drawn in heavy air. A mad tangle of kudzu vines chokes the hills, and the gray swamp bottom lurks beneath even green expanses of lawn, topped with white marble, black granite markers.

Washington. The afternoon air hung heavy; it moved through the small window of the compartment, damp and hot, speckled with ash. The train moved slowly, stopping and starting with jerks. Jo, her feet up on the seat, leaning against the wall, thought she could see the spike of the Washington Monument through the haze. Bert groaned.

"Nice nap?" she asked.

He struggled to sit up, his hands and feet tied tight. He scowled. "Bitch."

Jo shrugged and began to count her money. *Gotta get out of here.*

"Why do you keep whappin' me in the head?" Bert grumbled.

Jo glanced back. "Why do you keep bothering me?"

He rubbed his nose with his fists. "Shoot. Why not?" He yawned. "You young, you stupid, you got lots a' money on ya. 'Sides —" His eyes narrowed. "You got somethin' to hide. Anybody with somethin' to hide is an easy mark." He nodded to himself. "Always."

Jo frowned and listened at the door. *Someone coming.* Jo hoped it wasn't the conductor. "Guess I'm not so stupid right now, huh?"

Bert laughed. "Guess not." He chuckled to himself again. "Guess not," he said softly.

The train jerked forward again, and Bert boosted himself into an upright position. "Say, I got a bottle in my packet there. Can ya at least give a fella a little drink?" He gave Jo the look of a begging puppy, eyebrows arched hopefully. She thought for a minute, then shrugged. Why not? She dug the bottle from his pack and put it in Bert's hands. He took a long slug, choked and grinned again. "Maybe you're not so bad after all." He looked around. "You leave me in here and they'll put me in jail again, you know," he whined. She shrugged and he muttered, "Least I'll go in style."

Jo turned her back and stared out the window. The tracks passed through a shanty town, a Hooverville, and a few of the 'boes looked up and lifted their hands in greeting as the train passed. Jo scanned for the familiar mop of orange hair, an ordinary figure in dusty overalls. *Why did Max run away from me?*

"Ya know there's plenty a gals like you out here," Bert said, slurring slightly, to her back. "See 'em now and then. Heck, if it makes ya feel better, I prob'ly wouldn't a even guessed."

Jo wondered how far ahead Max was. *Wonder if he's thinking about me.*

"Now your pal, Max . . ." Bert started, reading her thoughts.

Jo turned, her throat constricting. "What? What about Max?"

Bert opened his eyes. "Ah, somethin' happened between ya, huh?" His bushy black eyebrows arched up oddly. "Where is your pal anyway? Fambly quarrel?" He snickered, and the sight of his brown snaggled teeth turned her stomach. She looked down and bit her lip.

"We were just friends." She looked toward the sound of laughter through the closed door, people passing in the corridor.

"Oh, yeah," Bert muttered, rambling on. "Most a the young guys head on home sooner or later anyway. New Yawk City, home. Reckon I oughta stop in and see my old woman myself . . . if she'll have me. See the fellers that's left on the block . . ." He paused, and then his voice raised. "Small world, ain't it, Josie?"

Jo watched the trees, big and leafy, different from

home, flashing past. Kids rode bikes and scooters or ran along the road, racing the train.

"From what Max told me," Bert mumbled, "we was practically neighbors. Small world, small world." Jo twisted to look at him, her heart beating faster. Bert grinned again, bleary-eyed. "Yup, I knew Max's pappy, Mick McCarthy, used t' drink with ole Mick . . ." Bert closed his eyes. He frowned, talking to himself, and opened one eye a slit to watch Jo. "Don't recollect he had no boy named Max, maybe a littler fella . . ." He breathed heavily and seemed to doze, but his lip curled in a sneer.

Jo pushed his arm. "Bert, wake up," she whispered. His eyes fluttered open.

"Josie," he said, slurring, and she sat back, away from the stale rush of his breath.

"You know where Max lives?" she asked, her heart thudding. Bert grinned and nodded. "Yup."

Jo smiled back at him and picked up his bottle. "How about another drink, Bert?"

"Care t' join me, Max?" Wit pulled a bottle from the darkness of her handbag and raised her eyes to meet Maxine's. "Or is it something else?" she asked, eyebrow lifting.

A blush tingled at the roots of Maxine's hair, and she looked down and grinned sheepishly. "Maxine," she said, her tone low. She turned it over on her tongue again, "Maxine."

Wit uncorked the bottle and took a long pull. Maxine saw the small thin hand reach out to her chin and felt it lifted. Slowly, she met Wit's eyes.

"You don't strike me no passing woman," Wit said frankly. "Nor one who's none too experienced neither, I reckon." Maxine felt warm under her quiet smile. "Take a drink, kiddo." Wit put the bottle in Maxine's hand.

The whiskey burned softly through her and settled in. She knew what Wit meant, thought of the women down in the Village she'd pass on the street, the ones she used to think were men until some feather of recognition would brush the backs of her knees and she'd have to stop and look back, catch herself watching the sharp crease of the trouser legs curving to the waist, the smooth neck above the collar and like as not, the frank grin as the passing woman glanced back at her. No, she supposed she wasn't like them, not quite.

She scratched her scalp through her shaggy hair and admired the smooth silk stockings Wit stretched out before her. Passing woman... "Sam," Maxine said suddenly. Wit laughed, a short, husky chortle. "Sam is a passing woman." Maxine felt like an idiot as soon as she said it. She looked down, fingered the denim of her overalls, and blushed.

"Now, Jo," Wit started, eyeing Maxine sideways.

Maxine blushed even more deeply, remembering Jo's easy swinging stride, the way her trousers cinched in her loose shirt, the pale, smooth neck above her collar. *Even I didn't guess she was a girl.* Wit chuckled again. Maxine took a long swig from the bottle and choked. Her eyes watered. She passed the bottle to Wit and studied her carefully. Her dress was plain but stylishly cut, her lipstick red, blurred now with drink, and her eyebrows arched and penciled. *As if she were an actress.* And Sam...

"That Jo is a fine one," Wit said, slurring a little, her eyelashes lowering. She licked her lips and looked slyly at Maxine. "Most wouldn't never guess 'bout that one."

"Forget Jo." Maxine felt her anger rising again. *Forget Josephine.*

Wit laughed. "Uh huh. Sure."

She saw the young father watching them, the young mother gathering her child closer. What do they see, she wondered. *Girl dressed as boy with a very womanly woman . . .* Maxine tried to imagine it. *Do they see me as girl or boy?* What did they see in her companion? She blushed and looked away.

"Not even Mother would guess about that one." Wit smirked.

"Mother of God," the man said. He looked down his long, straight nose, eyebrows arched almost to the brim of his hat, first at Bert, who held his bottle in his bound hands, then at Jo, tightening the knots, who felt the blush rising up her neck as quickly as her stomach plummeted to her knees.

"Tickets, please." She flinched at the conductor's voice down the corridor.

The man's mouth closed and his thin mustache twitched up in a slow smile. His eyes crinkled a little at the edges. "I just *love* a mystery," he whispered, put his finger to his lips and winked at Jo, then stepped back into the corridor, pulling the door nearly shut behind him.

Bert and Jo stared at the door, trying to hear the low voices. "The lady is quite indisposed at the moment," the man said. They heard the rustle of money. "I believe this will take care of it." Bert's eyes widened and he met Jo's glance. He raised his eyebrows in a question; she shrugged. The man stepped inside again, tipping his hat to the conductor. He took it off, brushed a speck of soot from his shoulder, placed the hat on the overhead rack and touched the umbrella in Jo's hands. "I believe this is mine," he said. She blushed again, loosened her still-tight grip and looked at her lap.

"I'm sorry to have disturbed you, sir," she said, her voice catching gruffly. "I'll just be going." She moved as if to get up.

"Nonsense," he said, his eyes twinkling blue. He touched her arm for a second too long and her skin burned. "I've paid your fare and now you must repay me with your charming company." He placed the umbrella beside a leather valise on the rack, rubbed his hands together briskly and sat down, tweaking the crease in his trousers as he did. He crossed one leg over the other and folded his hands in his lap. He looked them up and down.

Bert met his gaze for a long second, then snorted a laugh. The man sniffed and turned his attention to Jo.

He was not much older than she, in his twenties she guessed, wearing a well-made suit and polished leather shoes. The red silk of his tie glistened in the light. *What does he see?* Jo tried to imagine herself: soot-stained trousers, blue work shirt, battered Brogans, the old brown Fedora. Jo tried to meet his eyes, lazy blue under half-lowered lashes. The edge of his black mustache curved up with a smile. Suddenly uncomfortable, Jo blushed again and looked down.

Bert snorted again. "Where's yer balls now, young Jo?" he slurred, then burst out laughing.

The man glanced at Bert. "I must say," he said to Jo, "this is a very unpleasant person." He leaned forward a little. "I'm certain you had an excellent reason to tie him up," he coaxed.

"He robbed me!" Jo burst out. She ducked her head again, embarrassed, then remembered to lower her voice. "Back South. Got me drunk and stole my money."

"Ah, young farmer on the road . . ." the man began, his eyes dreamy, watching Jo through the slits. "Hardly more than a boy, a youth." Bert, just raising his bottle to his lips, choked. Jo shifted uncomfortably and shot him a sharp look. The man ignored him. "Going to?" He raised his eyebrows.

"Uh, North," Jo said. "New York."

Smiling, he continued, his voice softening. "On his way to the big city, to New York, to seek his fortune." He looked her up and down and licked the narrow mustache over his lip. "And what might you find there, ah, Joseph, was it?"

Jo smiled weakly. His gaze never left her, wandering her body then back to her eyes. *What does he want with me?*

"So wha's yer name?" Bert was drunk now, but Jo had a feeling he knew something she didn't. He poked her in her ribs. "He's a dandy feller, ain't he now?"

"Ah, you're quite right," the young man said, uncrossing his knees and bending forward to extend his hand to Jo. "Edward Masters." His hand was soft and his fingers long. Jo looked down. Her hand in his was tanned and dirty, the nails ragged. He held it for a long moment, bent close to her face. She glanced up, blushed furiously, then dropped her eyes. "Joe Lee," she said. He was acting like Rafe used to act when he wanted to be mushy. *How did he guess I'm a girl?*

Bert leaned over and they both drew back from his smell. "I'm Albert Moynihan," he said loudly. "What about me?"

"Yes," Edward Masters said. His eyes lingered a second on Jo, then appraised Bert again. "What about you? No doubt an honest man at heart, the working fellow beaten down by hard times. Unpleasant on the surface, and forced into a life of crime and wandering by circumstances, but a good soul, a kind heart —"

"He's a drunk and a thief," Jo snorted.

"No!" Bert shouted. "He's right. I ain't such a bad feller. I got a wife. I got little tykes. I used to be a good guy." He squinted at Jo. "You go ask your pal, Max. He'll tell you." His chin quivered. "I wouldn'ta hurt ya none." He started to blubber.

"Oh, brother," Jo said. "Now you've done it."

A red handkerchief appeared from Edward Masters' pocket. "I do hate to part with this," he said ruefully, then passed it to Bert, who took it in his tied hands, mopped at his eyes and blew his nose loudly. "No, no, please keep it," he said, when Bert tried to give it back. He rolled his eyes at Jo. "Some men."

Bert took another swallow from his bottle and closed his eyes.

"Smoke?" Edward reached into his jacket and pulled out a slim, silver case filled with tight, white machine-rolled cigarettes. Jo stared at them as he selected one. "Like beautiful young men," Edward murmured. Jo's eyes jerked to his face. He smiled. "The cigarettes," he said. "They look to me like beautiful young men in athletic togs, standing at attention." His fingertips brushed Jo's — intentionally, she thought — as he passed her the cigarette. They both stared at the flame from his lighter as he cupped it toward her. "Are you an athlete, Joseph?" Edward asked softly.

Jo blushed and sat back, inhaling her cigarette. Edward lit his own and snapped the lighter shut with a loud click. *Does he know I'm a girl?*

Bert began to breathe evenly, apparently asleep. Edward nodded toward him. "He's neither good nor bad, you know, Joseph."

Jo shrugged. She held her cigarette the way Jack did, between thumb and forefinger, and crossed her legs, ankle on knee. "If he's not good or bad," she said, "what is he?"

Edward smiled and exhaled blue smoke. "Ah, he's a character." He waved his burning cigarette out with a sweeping gesture. "An actor." The smoke arched. "A poor player that struts and frets his hour upon the stage."

"Macbeth," Jo murmured, then blushed as Edward arched his eyebrow. Jo looked out the window, trying to avoid Edward's blue gaze. So different from Max's, she thought, remembering the black ring, the way the pale lashes almost disappeared.

She started at Edward's hand on her knee. She looked into his eyes. "Not a simple country boy, then, Joseph?" he murmured.

The side track is a place of change, diversion, a backstage waiting room for the right switch, the right engine, the string of cars with a similar destination. The ordinary passenger in his Pullman car, comfortable in velvet cushions, clean and relaxed, glances up from his paper and gazes out the window, noticing the branching set of rails, curving away into dark green woods, dusty with rare use. He wonders where they lead, what is off the main line. He dozes into a place where nothing is as it seems and he is not sure who, or what, he is. The siding long past, he starts awake, afraid, shakes the thoughts back into imagination, straightens his tie, checks his ticket again, picks up the paper and reads. The song fades from the side tracks as the train rushes on.

My Gawd, you *are* a girl, ain't you now," Wit laughed. She stood back with her hand over her mouth as Maxine appeared from the underbrush, slow and blushing.

The clouds had parted just as they'd come into Philadelphia, and Wit, "stoppin' for a little shoppin' trip so's to be presentable for the city," had pulled Maxine off the train with her. "You don't want to show up at your mama's dressed like that," she said. And Maxine, looking down at her overalls, had to agree. "You stay here," Wit said, and parked her outside the department store window. "I'll take care a whatcha need," she assured her, and then she was gone. Maxine watched as Wit strode busily through the store, stroking the stockings, examining the heel on a shoe, checking the seams on dresses. "But you didn't get nothin'," Maxine protested when Wit came out and waggled her finger for her to follow. Wit had just smiled.

Now, standing between the tracks of the siding, Maxine knew that Wit had stolen the blue dress, the silk stockings and the leather shoes she was wearing. "All outta Wit's department store," Wit laughed, patting her handbag. "You look sweet, kid," she said. "That hair is a little short still, but it looks sorta fashionable for the city, I reckon."

"Mama won't like it," Maxine said, shrugging, then swirled the skirt out around her knees. It was strange to feel the air on her legs again, and she walked a couple of steps to hear the *shssh* of the stockings. Her breasts seemed to jiggle with every movement and she was suddenly cold. *It's like I've taken off my costume backstage. Or put one on.* She smoothed the fabric at her waist. *Which part will I play now?* "I've never had such beautiful clothes," she said. *Stolen.* "Thank you, Wit." She felt her skin go warm all over. Wit stood, cigarette dangling from her lip in concentration, fastening her stocking to her garter. She wore nothing else at all. Maxine blinked.

Wit stretched her arms over her head. "Like what you see, kiddo?" she asked, lowering her lashes.

Maxine dropped her eyes. Aside from her mother, she'd never seen a grown-up woman naked before.

Wit laughed. "I reckoned you'd go for a different kind."

Maxine forced herself to look up. "You're beautiful," she said, hearing the tremor in her voice.

Wit took her cigarette from her mouth. "Thanks."

Her breasts were small and round, the nipples dark, more brown than Maxine's. The dark hair where her legs met glistened in the sun. There was a long scar on the smooth skin of her hip. Maxine felt warm suddenly, dizzy. She sat down on a stack of railroad ties and closed her eyes. *Jo would have skin like that.* "You okay, kid?"

Maxine looked up and nodded. "I was just thinking about someone."

The brown eyes gentled. "Yeah." She nodded. "You got it bad, kid." She slid her own new dress over her head and smiled at Maxine as she buttoned it up. "Will Jo come lookin' for you, you think?"

Will she? Maxine wondered. She shrugged, her chest caving in to the place where the hot anger had been. *Why hadn't she stayed a boy?*

"If she don't, she's a fool," Wit said, looking her up and down appraisingly.

"I feel like I'm wearing a costume."

Wit came closer and took out a little jar. "Hold still," she said. "Let's make you up a little, honey." She dabbed color onto Maxine's lips, powdered her cheeks and then brushed her eyelashes with mascara. "Gotta complete the picture," she muttered and stood back. "Um, hum," Wit nodded. Maxine's face felt thick, covered. She wondered what her mother would see. "If your Jo don't come after you, then you come see me and I'll introduce you around." Wit winked at her. "Plenty to make you forget in my part of town." Maxine stood up, and Wit smiled. "Plenty'll want to *help* you forget too, you lookin' like that, kiddo."

She picked up her handbag and set off toward the main line again, hips swinging. Maxine glanced around at the green shadows, the rusty tracks and switchman's lever. A bright red, black-masked bird chirped loudly. She stepped carefully in her heels on the black ties, her hands brushing the skirt of her dress. This time she wasn't startled when her breasts moved. She smiled. *Maybe goin' home to New York isn't gonna be quite the same, maybe I just belong in another part of town.* Maxine stopped. *Maybe I'm not quite the same.*

"You never said exactly why you were going to New York, Joseph," Edward Masters said. "Business?"

Jo thought about the letter in her pocket. "Well," she began. "I have a letter to a lady." She looked up. "A Miss Corwin." Edward blinked, but his face remained smooth. "And there's someone else I need to find. A friend."

Edward sat up straighter. "Ah ha. A friend." He uncrossed his legs. "Now would that be a lady friend or a gentleman friend?"

Jo blushed. "Uh, just a fellow I traveled with for a while."

"And what is that fellow's name?" Edward's eyes were softer now.

"Max." Jo heard her voice catch and saw Edward's eyes lighten a shade.

"Ah ha," he said quietly. "A special fellow I think..."

Max. Jo looked out the window again, ignoring Edward, and took a long drag off her cigarette. Mama'd always said that boys didn't like girls who chased after them. Not that that'd ever been a problem, Jo thought. She leaned her face against the streaked glass and watched the passing woods through the rain. *Not till now, anyway.*

Jo started at a knock on the door. Edward's hand touched her knee and she jumped again. "Philadelphia, fifteen minutes!" came the conductor's voice. "Fifteen minutes to Philadelphia," he sang.

"The City of Brotherly Love," Edward murmured. He gave Jo one of his long, twinkling looks. He stood up and pulled his valise from the overhead rack. "Untie your friend Albert, will you, dear?" he said. "We have some work to do to carry off this little drama."

Jo moved to the seat opposite Bert's and fumbled with the ropes, watching as Edward opened his suitcase. "What do you mean?" she asked.

He began to rifle through the garments in the bag. "The conductor mentioned a little matter of some hoboes aboard the train." He glanced back at Jo. "Said one of them actually accosted a lady in the car just behind this one. Can you imagine?" He winked. "In any case, I think it would be in everyone's best interest if my dear mother here —" He nodded to Bert, who snorted once in his sleep. Edward shuddered. "If dear mother were allowed to sleep it off." With that, Edward pulled a black dress from his suitcase.

Jo's jaw dropped. He glanced at her.

"I'm an actor, of course, Joseph." He laughed. "Costumes, costumes, dear." He looked Jo up and down. "We'll have to spiff you up a bit too, I believe." His lazy smile and drooping eyelids rested on her just a little too long. "In fact, I think I have just the thing for you."

A memory of Sam and Wit, Max's voice echoed

behind Jo's ear, "Women like that, and men too, fellows dressed up like girls even." And Father's voice: "The devil's workshop." Jo blushed suddenly, the blood hot behind her eyes.

Bert snorted again in his sleep and they both glanced over at him. Edward sniffed, took off his jacket and placed it gently on the rack. He rolled up his shirtsleeves and began to unbutton Bert's shirt. "You'll find a nice blue suit in there, Joseph," he said. "I think you're about my size." He wrestled Bert's pants down and wrinkled his nose. "Oh my God." Jo looked up from the suitcase and swallowed hard at the sight of Bert's pasty white skin and hairy torso, Edward standing over him with his hands on his hips. "These working fellows," Edward murmured. "Too bad they never bathe . . ."

The fabrics in Jo's fingers felt regal. The blue slacks slithered like something alive, and she was nearly certain the shirts were silk. She didn't even know anyone who owned clothes so fine. *How the heck am I going to put them on here?*

"I don't think I need to change," she said. Edward was just rolling the veil of Bert's hat down over his face.

"Nonsense," he said, not looking up. He draped a lap blanket over Bert's knees and gently laced his fingers in his lap. Bert smacked his lips, snorted and then breathed evenly again. "There," he said. "The Queen of England." He leaned back to admire his handiwork and Jo couldn't help but laugh. Edward smiled at her. She scooted a little closer to the door. His eyelids lowered halfway again. "Maybe you need me to dress you too," he said, his voice huskier.

"Philadelphia!" came the conductor's cry. "Philadelphia next!"

Jo stood up clutching the blue suit and silk shirt. "No."

Edward turned toward her. His hand suddenly reached for her between the legs. "Do you dress right or left, sir-ir?" His voice changed and his brows knit as he grabbed her.

Jo gasped, wrenched open the compartment door and burst out, bumping into the conductor.

"Pardon," the conductor said.

Bert stirred, then belched. Edward gaped. Jo pushed past the conductor and into the corridor. As she fled she heard the conductor's voice: "Sorry to disturb you, madam . . . sir . . . uh, madam."

Jo stood in the open door of her boxcar, sweet with the scent of lumber, the fresh-cut boards stacked behind her still dusty from the mill, and watched the city snake closer. New York, its spikes glittering light in the setting sun, its crevasses dark in the setting sun. It moved, blurred, a place of migrating shadows, never still, never clear . . . *New York. The North. I'm gone now.*

Her hands were deep in the pockets of the fine smooth suit. Her hat was tipped back on her head and she'd buttoned the white shirt all the way up and tied the tie as best she could. She exhaled cigarette smoke into the wind and wondered about that strange fellow, Edward Masters. *He thought I was a boy . . . another kind of boy.* She shivered. *What am I, now? Maybe just another poor player on the stage.* She remembered what he'd said about Bert.

Bert. They'd have already made New York by now. She smiled to herself at the thought of Bert in his queen's dress. The setting sun cast the train's shadow long over the marsh grasses. The city skyline appeared again over the water. Jo hadn't been able to get a freight train out of Philadelphia for most of the afternoon and now she didn't know how she was going to find Max. Bert had been her link. She wondered how he would fare with Edward. What did either of them want with her, anyway?

She bit her lip, remembering her mother sitting on the hard wooden chair by Jo's bedroom door, her hands under her legs, her eyes lowered, blushing furiously under her powdered cheeks.

She remembered pricking up her ears as her mother had stumbled into, "And when you get married, your husband will, uh, well . . ." Jo had wanted to take her mother's hands and say "It's okay, you don't have to say it, I'll figure it out myself," but her curiosity — and her mother's contagious embarrassment — had kept her twelve-year-old mouth quiet. "That is," Mother had mumbled, "you'll be expected to, ah, well . . ." She had pursed her lips. "It won't be pleasant, but it's a wife's duty." Jo felt her brow wrinkling again just as it had back then. "The most important thing is that you must not allow a boy to take advantage of you before you are married," Mother had said earnestly, glancing up to meet Jo's eyes. "It's your most precious gift to your husband."

She thought of the dark church, Max, that kiss.

She crossed her ankles, suddenly warm between her legs, remembering. Something had been odd, different than kissing Rafe. *Max. Different.* She shook her head. The marsh grasses slanted back away from the train, the steam and smoke from the engine puffing out, dispersing into the clouds in the clearing sky like ghosts.

I wanted him to take advantage. She felt her cheeks and neck flame warm. *Dang, I wanted to take advantage of him.*

She thought of Edward Masters again, then Rafe. Both men, she thought, but different. *Both wanted me, not a girl who chases after boys, and I didn't want either of them.*

Jo felt tears well suddenly behind her eyes. *Must be something wrong with me.* She bit her lip. *Maybe that's why Max ran away.*

"You'll find somebody," Jack had said that last time they'd gone fishing. Jo pulled out her pouch and papers and turned her back from the door and wind to roll another cigarette. *Jack.* Jack, who'd be on his way to seminary by now. How she'd envied him his going — going somewhere, anywhere — and his knowing exactly where, and what, who, he was going to be. *And me . . .* She glanced over her shoulder to the New York skyline again. *There. Other places.* She smiled, her mouth twisting. *A preacher, at least, I'm not.*

Jo wondered how good a preacher her brother would be. "Some girls like doing it too," he had told her and Rafe on one of their fishing trips after he'd managed to get Becky Smith to walk out into the cornfield with him. Of course, he loved Becky. They were already engaged. "So it's 'most the same as if we're married," he said seriously. Rafe looked hard at her, but Jo just exhaled the smoke from her cigarette in a burst of laughter. "You'll find somebody too," Jack said.

" 'Less you're like that old dried up Miss Langley," Rafe crowed. She had laughed again then, swallowing something harsh. Miss Langley was her friend.

Somebody. Max. And now I've spoiled it. The cigarette calmed her tight chest and smoothed her brow. She watched the pale smoke drift slowly up into the boxcar and then sweep out, sucked by the draft, through the door and into the skyline.

Home. Maxine stood on the sidewalk across the street from her own brownstone stoop. A man pushing an apple cart passed slowly, his shoulders bent, the automobiles behind him honking and hiccuping exhaust. A gang of dirty kids played marbles in the long shadows of the buildings and she scanned the group for her siblings. They'd already be in to dinner, she guessed. They kept glancing up at her, whispering to each other, and she knew she stood out from the crowd of neighbors hurrying home, men in sooty work boots and women with sacks of carrots and potatoes. She almost wished her fine new clothes were tattered and stained. *And my hair.* She touched the short fringe of her bob. *Will Mother know me without my hair?*

Her skin felt grimy, the sweat of late afternoon beading in the corners of her eyes. Laundry hung like limp angels, their whiteness shackled between darkening buildings. *Maybe I don't belong here anymore.* But her feet had grown into the pavement. *I can't go away again.* She took a deep breath. *I am one of them. Family. I do belong.* She lifted her chin against the thoughts. *He'll beat me, Mother will turn away from me, the kids won't know me . . .* And she stepped out into the traffic, jaywalking across the street. *My home.*

Jo got off the motorbus, still stunned with the crush of people, the constant moving, the smells, the din, the lights. She clutched the letter from Miss Corwin in her sweaty hand and tried to move toward the street sign against the waves of shoulders and rushing feet. *This is sure different from home.* She longed for a map, the clear black lines and boundaries on flat white with neat folds, but her pockets were empty, her money gone. *Guess I'll have to find my own way.*

The fast thud of her pulse against the silky tie at her throat was reassuring. *I'm here. I'm in New York. It's not a dream.* The sign was useless, twisted on its post, and she stared up at it, circled it, craned her neck to see above the crowd. She felt dizzy with the aromas of food. I'll never find Bert or Max here, she thought. Jo sighed. She had resigned herself to finding Miss Corwin, to going off to college. *To never seeing Max again.*

A shoulder rammed hers, no "pardon me," jarring her out of her thoughts. *Everyone goes so fast here.* Indeed, when she asked a man directions, his words tumbled over themselves and into the streets and up into the spires of skyscrapers so fast that her head couldn't turn fast enough to follow them from his flailing hands. Not certain she really understood, she turned to thank him and he was already gone, another disappearing suit in the crowd. Jo shook her head and set off in the direction in which he had pointed.

The street was comparatively quiet. Trees lined its narrow walks and she could see glimmering chandeliers through the windows just above. Wealth showed itself. Jo wondered if she were really in the right place.

She rang the bell at the address that matched her envelope and a servant in a maid's black dress and white apron let her into an entryway. "I'll give this to Miss Corwin then."

Jo turned, startled. A man's voice? But the maid was already climbing the carpeted stairs, shapely legs in black stockings whispering as she — *he?* — climbed.

Jo caught a glimpse of herself in the ornate gold mirror beside the door. *Oh no.* Her hand went of its own volition to her tie. Caught up in the blur of city, she'd forgotten. *She expects a girl.* Jo panicked, her head pounded suddenly and sweat poured into her palms. She reached for the doorknob.

"Miss Corwin will see you now," said the deep voice.

Jo reluctantly let go of the cool handle. She inhaled a deep breath and followed the maid up the hall. The hips were decidedly narrow, but when the maid stepped aside to let her go first into the room, breasts pushed forward from her — *his?* — uniform. Jo

115

blushed as the maid stared frankly back at her, up and down. She — *he* — gave her a sly wink and nodded into the room.

Red and gold brocade curtains framed the huge window overlooking the street. A streetlight just beyond blocked Jo's clear view of the figure standing there. Blue smoke drifted lazily upward, and Jo smelled a cigar. A man in a suit turned, nodded to her, and began to walk around the side of the piano.

"Oh," Jo began. "Excuse me sir, but I'm here to see Miss Carlotta Corwin. The maid . . ." Jo faltered.

"Carlotta Corwin," said the man, his voice a woman's, melodic and low. *But a woman's.* She held out her hand to Jo. *Her hair is long.* "Carl to my friends."

Jo felt her mouth open and close, but no sound came out.

"You must be Josephine," she said. She took Jo's hand and wrapped it under her arm to lead her to a sofa. "Priscilla — Miss Langley — said you were an unusual girl. But I didn't quite expect this." She waved her cigar at Jo, still holding her hand. "Not from a Southern preacher's daughter."

Jo blushed and was glad for the dusky lamp shade of the room's only light. "I don't usually dress like this," she mumbled. "I mean, I can explain. I, I've been, um, traveling . . ."

"Oh, I know you have," Carl said, laughing huskily. Her brown hair settled shining and thick around her man's collar and necktie. She wore a gold watch chain draped across her vest . . . *breasts.* "And I want to hear all your stories," she said. "But let me look at you." She dropped Jo's hand and draped an arm across the sofa back. "Quite the queer bird, aren't you?"

Jo didn't know what to say. The way the woman said it, it was almost like praise. "Um, yes, uh, ma'am. I suppose so." Her tongue felt thick and her neck itched. She wasn't used to people looking at her like that. *Through me, into me, all of me. Not like that.*

Carl shook her head sadly. "Well, we'll have to do some shopping before we send you off to Massachusetts. Though I suppose you'll find some occasions for drag up there still."

The room seemed to be getting warmer, the shadows closing in, and Jo felt herself sway on her feet a little. *I'm dressed as a man. She's dressed as a man.* She blinked several times quickly, the white spots changing to black spots before her eyes. Everything seemed to be shadows.

"Oh, where are my manners," Carl said, rocking to her feet. "You must be exhausted. Let's get you to a bath, and my husband will be happy to take you shopping tomorrow, I'm sure." The small strong hand took Jo's arm again. *Husband?* She looked into Carl's glittering brown eyes. "Everything will be clearer tomorrow." She smiled, ringing for the maid. "This is David," Carl said as he came in. He dropped into an exaggerated curtsy, spreading the hem of his uniform dress and white apron, his stockinged leg and black pump stretched back. Carl laughed. "He'll show you to your room, but I doubt he'll make anything clear."

Steam rose from the flat, silver looking glass of water in a smooth gray wave of fog. It soaked through pale skin into invisible pores, loosened microscopic bits of black grime, blanched dead skin, sweated them out to be washed away into the bath, *like a baptism.*

Jo closed her eyes but images kept flashing behind her lids — David, the maid, his shushing stockings, his wink at her; Carlotta . . . Carl . . . laughing through cigar smoke, the drape of the watch chain below the swell of her breasts, "husband"; and her own reflection, the silk tie and blue suit, in the entryway mirror. Max's blue eyes. *Don't think.* She slouched farther into the hot bath; nothing had ever felt so good. *Let the steam make you blank. Nothing, no one in particular.* Her eyes opened and she smiled, remembering that long-ago Sunday morning, sitting in that open boxcar, cane pole beside her, touching the letters in her pocket and thinking, "I am not an ordinary one."

She looked at her body, distant and distorted by the wavering bath water. It had been so long since she'd seen her body, it was almost unfamiliar.

I am not an ordinary one. She thought of her father and mother, of Jack, and felt a pang like hunger high in her throat. "You are an embarrassment to your family," Father had said. *He meant I was not an ordinary one.* Jo bit her lip and felt sweat beading in the corner of her eye. All the things he'd said, all that she had learned and believed — *the black and white of the world* — seemed to have vanished into wisps and shadows.

She breathed the fog, deep into her lungs, imagining it spreading into her blood, beating in her heart. *Blank. Gray.* She settled into the water. *Nothing had ever felt so good.*

Maxine rubbed her youngest sister's head vigorously with the thin towel, and the little body danced and muffled giggles erupted. "Be a good girl for your big sister now," their Mother called from the kitchen. Maxine smiled to herself. *I belong here. Family.* Had anything ever felt so good?

She slipped the nightgown over her sister's head and hugged her tight. He was gone. Mick, her step-father, had miraculously disappeared like so many

119

others, wandering out into the night, pushed away by the shame of hard times, joblessness, or pulled perhaps by the call of road, the yearning song of the rails. Maxine didn't care. He was gone. And Patrick was up North, working in the mills, and Cousin Nat had a job for her too, her mother had said, if she wanted it, in his butcher shop. "I think he's sweet on you," her mother had confided. Maxine had stifled her shudder, the thought of his thick, cold hands. *Jo's fine long fingers, the night she had cut herself playing mumblety-peg* . . . She shook her head sharply. *No. She wouldn't want me if she knew I were a girl.* "We kin all go together, now," her mother had said, her eyes soft. "Make ourselves a new home." A home, Maxine thought. *Like everyone else. A family.*

"Quite the day 'round here," her mother called conversationally from the kitchen. "You here, and a bit of a stir down to Moynihans' too." Maxine began to scrub the backs of the two little ones still in the tub, ducking back as they splashed her, the littlest one standing behind her stroking her short hair. She felt soothed by the steady rhythm of clank and squeak, her mother ironing the clean laundry she took in from the rich ladies uptown. "Seems Albert Moynihan came home today too," she said, and Maxine stopped still, her hands clutching the washcloth under the warm water. Her mother laughed. "Came home stinking drunk, of course." She snorted. "Like somebody else I know. Sweet Jesus, I hope *he* don't decide to come home afore we can get out of here."

Maxine swallowed and remembered that night in the rain when she'd first met Jo. "You really think you killed him?" Jo's eyes had been wide and those long lashes dark shadows in the boxcar. It was hard to think of that pretty boy as a girl though. Maxine had recognized Bert long before then but had held her tongue. She didn't know if Bert would recognize her now... *a girl*... but she knew she'd have to keep out of his way.

"The oddest thing about Moynihan, though," Mama added. "He got out of a taxicab of all things, and already paid for, mind you." She laughed again, her ironing board squeaking. "And the poor fellow was wearin' a dress."

A board in the stair squeaked, but the figure at the window didn't turn. Jo felt as if all her insides were hollow, and she vaguely knew she needed to eat, but all she really wanted after the steam-cleaning of her bath were clean pajamas and the feather bed at the top of the stairs. Her limbs hung loose in the silk shirt and blue pants, and the effort of keeping her head upright on her neck was exhausting. "Carl?" she said, hesitant to break the calm smoky silence. She felt like a little child. "Carl, may I borrow a nightgown, please?"

Edward Masters turned from the window and smiled. "My dear Joseph."

Jo felt dizzy, and she sat down hard on the steps before she fell. She took several deep breaths, resting her head on her knees, her eyes closed. *I'm losing my mind.*

A warm hand touched her shoulder and she opened her eyes to see Edward's shining leather shoe on the step below. "Are you quite all right, my dear?" His voice was gentle, and when she looked up, he smiled kindly. "I am sorry to have shocked you." He took her arm and helped her down to the sofa, where he put her feet up before pulling the servants' bell and settling into an armchair. "My wife, Carl that is . . ." Jo felt her mouth gape again. "Oh just for appearances." Edward smiled. "Carl told me that her little protegé had arrived," he said. "But I had no idea it was you."

"David," he said, turning toward the shush of the maid's stockings. "Oh, get yourself out of that ridiculous outfit," he said, taking David's hand.

David grinned down at him. "Okay, boss." He kissed Edward lightly on the mouth, patted his cheek and walked out.

"And get Josephine something to eat too, dear."

Jo had never seen men kiss on the mouth. She felt her cheeks growing warm and closed her eyes again.

"I do apologize for that little embarrassment on the train," Edward said. He nudged her foot. "Smoke?" She sat up and took a cigarette from the silver case. "You do drag exceptionally well, my dear," he said, meeting her eye as the flame burst up from the lighter.

"Drag?"

Edward laughed. "Oh, you are a bit of the simple country lad, aren't you?" He gestured to her clothes with his cigarette. "You know, the 'clothes make the man' bit."

Wearing a woman's dressing gown, David came in with a silver tray and chimed in, "Or the lady!"

Edward grimaced. "You." He pointed to David. "I'll deal with you later." David put his hands over his mouth in mock fear, and Jo smiled in spite of herself. She stubbed out her cigarette and helped herself to a sandwich. "Speaking of which," Edward continued, his arm lazily rubbing David's back as he perched on the arm of Edward's chair, "your chum Albert must have made quite a stir upon his arrival home."

Jo stopped chewing. *Max.* Edward's eyes twinkled. She tried to swallow all at once.

"The queen," he dropped his voice to a whisper, "quite tipsy, I might add, returned home to the Lower East Side today in style."

Jo grinned. "In that dress?"

Edward nodded. "I got him smashed in the train after your abrupt departure . . . with its accompanying unsettling revelation . . ." He frowned and winked, and Jo blushed again. "And he slurred out all manner of thrilling adventure tales." Edward leaned forward. "Your friend, Max," he began.

Jo sat up straight. "Max?" Suddenly college was far away again and the city of shadows seemed to close in.

Edward smiled and drew his words out. "You are, I believe, as my spouse would say, silly for this Max. Am I correct?"

Jo dropped her eyes. *Silly?* It was a girl's word, but she couldn't ignore the feeling in her chest, the sensation in her stomach. *Max.* She slowly nodded. "I need to see Max again," she mumbled, almost to herself.

"Umm," David said quietly. "Young love."

She glanced up to find his sharp face smiling and his eyes crinkled at the edges, kind. Edward smiled too and gave her the address.

* * * * *

The top-floor apartment on East 1st Street was tiny, clothes and linens hanging every which way from lines drawn across the rooms. The air was steamy and the walls close, and Jo could hear people's voices and footsteps on the dark hall stairway and through the thin walls. It was so different from the apartment she'd just left, Carl's, and from her father's parsonage, too. The streets and lights, trains, automobiles, the noise and dirt, the people, all seemed to leave marks behind her eyes. She had blurred one shadow to the next, everything shifting. *I can see every shadow, and nothing is as it seems.* A little girl peered at her from the doorway through which Max's mother had just passed.

"I'll get Maxie then," Mrs. McCarthy had said after letting Jo in. She had looked Jo up and down, taking in the expensive blue suit, the neat silk tie. "I'm sorry for the mess, sir," she had murmured, dragging in two wooden chairs from the kitchen.

Jo touched her tie. She hadn't thought, hadn't even hesitated when Edward had given her Max's address. She'd grabbed the blue jacket and her shoes at a run, Edward pressing money into her hand while David held the door. The night had been too much for her to think anymore. She had just needed to see Max one more time, just to know there was at least one boy she could like. *Maybe even love.*

"A fine young fellow," Jo heard. "How do you know such a rich boy?" *Am I a rich boy now?* The voices were low. She smiled at the little girl, who giggled, her freckles wrinkling on her nose as Max's did, and ducked back through the doorway.

Max. The blue eyes at the doorway widened and pink spread to the roots of red hair. Max's mother pushed, and they both walked into the room. Max wore a blue dress, the color of her eyes. *Gosh, I didn't know he had a twin sister.*

"Hullo, Jo," she said in Max's voice.

Jo felt the breath disappear from her lungs. *A girl!*

Maxine stumbled, and her mother's hand in the small of her back pushed her forward again. Jo's face had gone blank, colorless. Maxine felt the heat of her own face like it was on fire. "It's me," she said, her voice quavering.

Jo stood up. She opened and closed her mouth a couple of times.

"Sit down, please," Mama said. Jo looked around wildly, first at Mama, then to the door, then back at Maxine's legs again.

Jo blinked. "No, ma'am, um," she started. She looked at the older woman. "No, you sit down." She shook her head sharply and stepped away from her chair. "Please."

Maxine saw her mother's small smile as she sat in the chair Jo offered. She sat down herself, stiff, her knees watery.

"You're different," Jo said suddenly.

She hates me. Maxine swallowed.

"Oh," Mama jumped in. "Everyone is different in their home, amongst their own."

Jo's green eyes stared into Maxine's. "Yes," she said. "Family."

"And where are you from, Mr. Lee?" Mama asked, a note of excitement in her voice. "Not from around here, I'm sure." Maxine suddenly realized that her mother thought Jo was a beau, a suitor. She felt her blush rise to her ears again.

"Jo is just a friend I met while I was traveling, Mama."

"Now let Mr. Lee talk, Maxine," Mama replied.

Jo blinked again at the name. She cleared her throat. "I'm from the South, Mrs. McCarthy," she said, her voice lower now. "On my way to college." She didn't take her eyes off Maxine.

"College," Mama said, awe in her tone. "And handsome too." She touched Maxine's hand.

"Mama," she started, her voice warning.

"Look at those long eyelashes," Mama said. Jo's face turned ruddy. "Wasted on a boy," she cajoled.

Jo felt herself smile. "My mother says the same thing," she said. She touched her tie again nervously.

She looked down at her shoes and then at Max again. *A girl. Maxine.* The familiar eyes, the black rings wider around the blue, met hers, pleading. A lock of the short red hair had sprung from the scarf over her head and brushed the pale brows. Jo remembered that night Max had saved her from Bert.

"Maxine," Jo heard herself say aloud. She was beautiful. *Different. A girl.* Jo shook herself. *A girl.* Her breath caught in her chest again. "I, uh, I've got to be going," she said suddenly, and she bolted out the door.

Liquid and soft, the night air caressed her. The yellow of the moon, swollen with waiting, brushed the soft hairs at her nape, smoothed the exhaustion in her eyes. The mists and shadows nipped at her heels and slithered, cool, up the seams of her silk stockings, the backs of knees shivering. An ancient, restless warmth settled in her bones, like the fog thickening near the shacks jumbled together beside the web of rails. Fragments of old lives, she thought, old rules and ways, and the sharp bite of new tin and window panes lined with silver cracks.

Maxine stumbled as her heel caught the rail of a side track. *I can't let her go like this.* She stopped and searched the gloom for Jo's back, hurrying, hunched, into the dark. She had been just ahead, there, and now she was gone, faded into the shadows. *She can't just disappear . . . she's not that way.*

Jo leaned back against the outside of an empty boxcar, alone on the siding, and watched the moon, full again. Yellow. It had been a yellow moon the night she left home, the air thick with possibility, sweet. But here, the air creaked and rustled, cloaked her shoulders with heavy river smells. Light flickered, dancing neon under her wrists. *Maybe I should try to disappear.*

The moon's light was weird, neither bright nor dim, changing as fogs and clouds danced in and around it, and she saw not a face, but the shadows of the moon's terrain, peaks and crevasses.

Max . . . Maxine. Jo tilted her head back against the warm wooden wall and closed her eyes. The two faces, boy and girl, blurred. The blue-and-black eyes, skin the color of pale Georgia peaches, the shock of hair . . . The way the small fingers had curled up into her palm, stroking lightly, when she had cut herself that night . . . the tingling in her hand.

It's not right. She's a girl. I'm a girl. Not the way it's supposed to be. The boxcar swallowed the echo as Jo thumped her head back against the wall. *Dang.*

She reached in her pocket and took out the silver cigarette case Edward had put there as she had run out.

"Young love," David had said. Jo thought about Edward's arm around David's back. Their kiss. She remembered Sam, at the Hooverville near Richmond, the way she had kissed Wit, the way their bodies had curved together.

As Jo smoked, her shoulders relaxed into the rough warmth of wood, and she felt the stiffness in her neck dissolve into the night air. *"Young love."*

Voices rose up, rough and sour, from the shacks, and Bert looked toward them, toward the lights. His eyes gleamed yellow in the moonlight, and he staggered a little, the nearly empty bottle clinking in the pocket of his dress. There were faint smudges of blush on his cheeks, his eyes were outlined in black and the red lipstick smeared into a clown-mask around his mouth.

"Saw 'em come this way," he muttered, stopping to catch his breath. He'd followed the both of them from where McCarthy lived, down to the switching yard, the river. "Make a fool outta me, will ya?" he grumbled. The lights and voices from the jungle drew his attention again. He scanned the dark once more, then spat on the dirt and wiped his mouth, smearing the lipstick some more. "Dykes."

Jo saw her, limping in her heels along the silver tracks. She smiled, remembering Max in his overalls, the easy way he had swung up to a boxcar by the iron rungs, the eyes grinning back at her, his hand reaching . . . *Her hand.* It made sense now, the thickness under Max's shirt as she'd boosted him along outside of Richmond. Jo touched her own binding. She hardly thought of it anymore. The girl, *the woman,* looked lost, her silhouette dark against the yellow moon. *Those curves ... How could I have not known?*

The shoulders sagged and Maxine drew her arms across her chest, hugging herself. A train called, the song rolling in from far away, and Jo's soles itched in response. Max seemed to be a million miles away, almost in some other land. *But she shouldn't be here alone.*

Jo pushed herself slowly away from the boxcar, her palms brushing the rough wood, and stepped away from the shadow into a yellow light.

A film of sweat on her palm, Maxine tried not to swing her legs, to be perfectly still, and smelled the smoky night scents of Jo. In the empty boxcar, the air held the scents of ripened fruit, flour, new-sawn wood in perfect stillness, holding the leftover day in the night, waiting. They sat, shoulders not quite touching in the open door, neither speaking, the quiet like a vacuum, the city holding its breath. *What can I say?*

Words skittered somewhere behind her ears, but there seemed to be nothing right, no script. The moon slipped a little lower toward the river.

"I —"

"I —" Jo stopped as Maxine spoke at the same moment. They glanced at each other, smiled and looked down. Jo felt something rushing in her forehead. *I don't know what to do.* Their hands lay warm and damp together, and her arm had numbed with the effort of not moving. "I didn't know you were a girl," she said quietly, and then stopped, not breathing. *Dumb, it sounded dumb.*

"I know," Max said, her voice sad. "I was afraid." Jo glanced over again. Max was talking to the ground. "When you, when we . . ." She paused and took a breath. "That night in the church, when you told me. I thought you would hate me if you knew." The eyes were almost black when they met Jo's. "I think I hated you." Max looked quickly down again. "I was afraid of what it made me."

Jo felt her forehead furrow. "What do you mean?"

"You know," she whispered. She looked down, her eyelashes fine and pale against her cheeks. "Dyke."

The back of Jo's neck burned, and she looked down the side of the boxcar toward the flickering lights in the shanty town. The word sounded flat, as if it were typed, the name of a place, perhaps, a marker, a tiny spot on a map. *What does it mean?*

"You were different," Max said softly, wondering. "Even after you said you were a girl, I loved you."

Love? Jo felt her throat close. She tried to swallow.

Maxine inhaled sharply. "I mean, um, I still wanted . . . wanted to be with you." Max's hand seemed warmer, sweatier. Jo snuck a look. Even in the dim light, Max . . . Maxine seemed flushed. *I don't know what to do.*

* * * * *

131

Maxine's chest was hollow, empty. She couldn't breathe anymore. *Why doesn't she say something?* Her tongue felt thick.

Jo sighed and Maxine felt the shoulder next to hers shift straighter. Their hands slipped a little. *She'll leave now.* Maxine inhaled and closed her eyes, but Jo's fingertips stopped short and rested, curled into her knuckles. Something tingled.

"It's not right," Jo said slowly, her voice heavy and faraway.

No. Maxine felt a fist press into the backs of her eyes.

Jo took a deep breath. "That's what my father would say." Maxine's lungs burned as if a coal were there, orange in a strong gust. Jo turned toward her, but Maxine couldn't move. "But I reckon I've got to make up my own rules," Jo said. Maxine's breath released, like the sigh of homecoming. She looked slowly over. Jo stared out across the maze of tracks and murmured, "Make my own map."

The green eyes met hers, the shadows of Jo's lashes like brush-stroked lines through the faint freckles across her cheeks. *I want to settle in here forever.* Maxine blushed, and looked down.

She heard Jo move, then warm breath stirred the fine hairs at her neck. Maxine shivered and sat still. She studied the line of Jo's nose, her jaw and her lips, trembling and vulnerable.

I don't know what I'm doing. Jo rested her face in the brush of Max's hair and breathed in rose water, the scents of children, ironed cotton, and something tangy, like ripened oranges, mixed with the flour dust in the boxcar.

Maxine's fingers began to stroke the inside of her palm, sparking. She heard the rustle of fabric and then blood rushed from the place where Maxine put her hand above her knee and pressed her thigh. *Who is she? Who am I?* A sound pushed through her lungs and she heard herself groan, the sound of freight shifting around a bend.

Jo found Max's mouth, held the soft curve of her jaw in her hand and fell into her taste, the texture of peach-smooth skin, the yield of lips like warm rain. *No map, no lines for this.* She closed her eyes, losing herself into scent, smell, touch. *Have to find my own way.*

Maxine felt herself settling, like lying back on a familiar feathered bed, into the sensation of Jo. Her tongue reached through, searching of its own will in the lush shadows for the place it belonged. It touched Jo's, and she felt the heat of the boxcar on her nape, sweat trickling between her breasts, like a dark hearth of coals glowing under her clothes. Their mouths seemed then alive, hungry, and they struggled on without breathing, dizzy, drunk. *Here is my home, in this gray.*

Her hand on Jo's thigh slid higher, following the long muscle, settling in the curve where leg met hip. She squeezed gently, then slid her fingers lower into the dark, damp fold of linen between her legs. Head full, ears humming, she found Jo's smooth neck with her other hand, slid through the fine fringe of hair, and unknotted the silk tie.

Jo gasped, her head falling back, as Max's teeth touched her collarbone, cool suddenly, exposed to the damp night air. Her own fingertips began to travel, searching, following the terrain of skin — thin weave of fabric, round swell of breast, the hard peak of a nipple. Maxine shuddered, and Jo knew that this was *it*, the *it* that men and women did. *But something else, some other road.*

Trembling, slow, they kissed again. Her nipple seemed to quiver, raw, waiting for Jo's hand again, jutting harder against the cotton of her dress with every thud of heartbeat.

Maxine unbuttoned Jo's shirt, her fingers stiff, fumbling. From Jo's thumb to her nipple, the moan, guttural and deep, exploded into her chest, her belly, her groin. She pulled Jo back with her into the boxcar, her spine jellied, her knees trembling.

The moonlight lay in a yellow square on the wooden floor. Cloud-draped, the light seemed to be coming through a lace-curtained window, an empty home. The necktie whistled as she pulled it through Jo's collar, and slipping the jacket and shirt off, she unwound the tired binding.

* * * * *

Jo's skin felt transparent, like the onion skin of her old map. It was as if her knapsack had been stolen, her compass, her lock of hair neatly tied in a blue ribbon. And it was also as if she had been freed. She knelt on a flour sack and looked at the white skin, the small breasts, the swell of her narrow waist. *Who am I now?*

She reached up, watched her long hand disappear into the shadow of Max's dress, and her palm stroked, unsteadily, up the smooth of stocking into the steam of skin, the wilderness she knew and did not know.

It was as if she were being rocked, dreaming and not dreaming, in some house, docked in a safe, gray harbor, a part of the storm, no longer alone.

It was as if she were a nomad, an explorer, with no way to regain her bearing, no marker but skin, scent, smell, and the cry that was herself, and was also someplace else.

This is where I belong.
This is a place where I am.

The jungle rambled, ragged and uneven, against the skyline of white granite, stone, the straight black lines of buildings, monuments, steeples. The pieced-together homes at this place where roads and rails converged, diverged, the mishmash of shacks and tents and bedrolls on the ground, rustled and groaned, and the yellow moon set into the thick river, cloud-shrouded, as if on stage a tattered curtain had begun to fall. The side tracks were wet with dew, gray in the shifting light, the boxcars scattered, empty, awaiting new freight, new destinations, the tricks of the switchman.

Maxine held Jo's hand tight, steadying herself as they walked between and across the web of tracks.

The night mists were thinning, but clouds hung low over the setting moon. She remembered leaving Richmond, the morning the sun didn't rise, and gripped Jo's hand tighter. *Wandering in the gray.* She glanced over at Jo, the long, straight jaw, the long eyelashes, the fine blue linen suit, the silk necktie she had knotted and straightened herself. *I'm home.*

"I'll walk you home," Jo murmured. She thought again of the night, the scent of flour, the warm boxcar.

"Be my husband," Max had said.

Jo felt a tremor crawl up her thighs toward her belly as she remembered. "What?" she had said.

"We can get married," Max had whispered.

Jo thought of her mother: *"Boys don't like girls who chase after them."* Jack: *"You'll find someone."* Edward: *"Silly."* Even Bert: *"Be a man."*

She remembered herself in the mirror that moonlit night she had run away, her hair cut short. "The man is the head of the woman." *What am I now?*

Max took her hand, touched her chin, turned her face toward her own. *Those eyes.* Jo felt herself swirling down into the vertigo of that black-ringed blue whirlpool.

"No one will ever know," Max had said. "You can pretend. You know you can." She had kissed her hungrily, her lips bruising Jo's.

The hum in Jo's ears grew to a roar and she heard again the sound that welled from her chest. She had rolled on top of her lover's lush body, a thin sweat separating their skins, and pushed herself deep inside.

A train whistle called, long and low through the gray, dissipating into the fog. *What am I now?*

They passed into the Hooverville, stepping carefully around the hoboes who slept in the open air, following the meandering dirt path between shacks, toward the sound of voices, the light of a fire and the city beyond. Maxine stroked Jo's hand with her thumb. She knew she had to go home; Mama would be worried. She felt the tingle again in her hand. *But this is where I belong.*

"Get the hell out of here, you fairy!" The rough voice was followed by a scuffle and thud. Bert fell into the firelight, his legs pale and white as the dress flew up. Several men laughed, harsh, and their shadows closed in around him.

Jo hesitated, then started forward again, Maxine's fingers grasping hers.

"No," Max whispered. "Let's go back."

Someone kicked at Bert, and she could see his face, smeared with paint, tighten with pain, his eyes wide and scared.

She wrenched her hand free. "We can't," she said, looking hard into the blue of Maxine's wide eyes. "*I* can't." Jo stepped into the light. "Leave him alone," she said, her voice gruff, tough. Her heart pounded against the binding Maxine had rewound. It cut under her arms, too tight. The burly man who had kicked Bert looked up, surprised, and took a step back.

She bent over Bert and took his arm. "Come on."

"Get your hands off me, dyke." Bert's eyes were glazed, hard and narrow. He cast his glance to the three other men. "Them," he nodded at Jo and Max, who took a step back from the light. "They did this to me," he snarled. "It's them you want."

The ringleader's thick neck bulged. His small eyes narrowed and his leer raked over Jo, then Max. Max shook her head vigorously and glanced back into the dark. The burly fellow looked back at Jo.

"Bull dagger, look at her," Bert said, raising himself to his knees in the dirt. Jo stared hard at the men, one by one, and tried not to blink.

"No," came a quiet voice, hard and deep from between the ragged shacks. "She's my sister." Jack — *Jack, my brother!* — stepped into the circle, huge, his shoulders wide and square.

Jo felt her jaw hanging open. *What is he doing here?*

Jack spoke, his eyes on Jo. "She's not a dyke."

Maxine's head swiveled to look at the man. His green eyes flickered in the light. Long dark lashes brushed his cheekbones as he blinked, and she looked back to Jo, back to him. *The same, and not the same.*

"Yes," Jo said softly, staring at the tall man. "Yes, Jack, I guess I am."

Max felt her breath burning in her lungs. She wanted to run, fade into the dark, to go home.

Bert coughed, bending over to the ground again, and spat, the crimson of blood staining the dirt. The rough, thick-necked man who had kicked him looked over and snorted. He glanced again at Jo, at Max, then at Jack, took his measure, and stepped back from the fire.

Jo touched Bert's shoulder again, and this time he looked up, hesitating. " 'Blessed are ye when men shall revile and persecute you,' " she murmured, glancing back at Jack.

It's not just hair.

Jo watched the barber's scissors in the mirror, his hands soft and unsure, his face puckered, frowning. The shears stuttered a *sh-sh-sh*, marking, and obscuring. Her head appeared as the hair fell away. Light gleamed at the uneven line of the part. "You don't want me to cut more?" he said, his voice wavering, unbelieving. He still looked horrified. Edward laughed, and Jo glanced at his grinning reflection in the mirror, then nodded.

Her gaze slid to Maxine, who sat clutching the bags and boxes of the morning's shopping trip, her eyes, like those sidelong glances of the men waiting around her, worried, confused. Her lips were tight. *She's still mad.*

Max had gasped and grabbed Jo's arm when she started in, past the striped barber pole. "You can't," she said. Scared, she looked around at the people passing, through the window where the men sat waiting.

Jo shrugged her off. "I want a proper haircut," she said, and after Edward took the shocked barber aside, money changing hands, she sat in the barber chair, tucking her dress under her neatly, met the blue-and-black eyes in the mirror, then the nervous barber's and said, pointing to Jack, who had come along, "Like his. Short."

The barber finally finished, brushing her neck with a soft whisk, shaking his head, and untied the cloth around her neck.

Jo stood and examined her reflection, turning to see the back of her head, the hair even and slicked down, very short. Her long and barely curved figure was draped in a summery dress, the high waist and low neck accenting her small bust. She touched the tiny buttons, twisted to see the skirt flair out. Its brush at her knees sent an unfamiliar shiver up the backs of her legs. *Who am I now?* She smiled.

"You look like a boy in a dress," David observed.

"Like me in a dress," Jack said, his eyebrows arching. "Like Joan of Arc."

"It would look much better on me." David winked.

Flushed, Maxine hurried outside and waited for them on the sidewalk. "Why did you have to do that now?" she asked when Jo joined her. "You could have waited until you were back in pants."

Jack touched Max's arm. "Because this is who she is," he said. Jo looked at him. "You can see her now," he said. "All of her."

Maxine's eyes were very pale, the black ring around the blue seemed wide. The blush had settled into her jaws, and her mouth was tight.

"You want me to be parts," Jo said quietly.

The three men walked on ahead, Jack's swagger exaggerated next to the other two. Jo remembered again to walk slow, to shorten her stride and swing her hips more than her shoulders. Mother and Father had sent him to look for her. *Who will he tell them he'd found?* She reached to take Max's hand.

Maxine wrung herself free and crossed her arms over the packages, glancing around anxiously. "You can't do that," she hissed.

Jo thought for a second, the tap of her heels matching Maxine's pace. "Have I changed?" she wondered aloud. She glanced at Max. "Aren't I the same person I was last night?"

Maxine was silent.

"Aren't I the same hobo you kissed in that church?" Jo said. They turned the corner toward Carl's West Village apartment, and her heel caught on a crack in the walk. She stumbled into Max.

The packages flew from Maxine's arms as she and Jo lurched onto the stoop of a brownstone. Jo

143

grabbed at the railing, grabbed at Maxine's arm, and Maxine slid to her hip, her palm burning on the concrete. Jo's legs were tangled in hers, and her dress had flown up to show her cotton slip and her long, curving leg. She righted herself and smoothed her hem, gathering up the packages. Watching her, Maxine licked the red scrape on her hand. *It's as if she doesn't care.*

Jo took her hand. "I'm sorry," she said, opening the palm. "That looks like it hurts."

Maxine stared at the top of her gleaming hair — *a man's haircut.* Jo bent down — *at the knee, like a woman* — to examine the scrape. *How can I be with her like this?* But Jo's hand was kind, her fingertips tingled where Jo stroked them. "You *are* different," she heard herself say.

Jo stood up. The green eyes met hers, the long cool fingers still holding her smarting hand. Jo nodded, slow and serious, and then she leaned in and kissed her, long and slow, on the mouth.

Jo felt Maxine's body yearn toward her, like last night was crushing in, then she stiffened and pushed Jo back hard. "You can't do that here." She looked up and down the street and Jo followed her glance. A woman with a baby carriage passed on the other side, staring, frowning at the two of them. "What will people think?" she whispered.

Jo sat down on the lower step, tucking her skirt under her legs. She rested her chin in her hands, silent for a long moment, all the places she had been, the people and things she had seen, shifting. No one seemed to be in the same place, the right place. *Except inside me. I am in my own place.* Maxine rustled behind her. *What do people think? Where does anyone feel?*

Finally she murmured, "I don't know."

The scream of a steam whistle wandered out into the canyons and shadows, the dark alleys and bright skyscrapers of the city. Jo stared through the window of her car onto the platform, imagining the grumble of automobiles and the shouts of street vendors outside, silent for a second, listening for random bits of train song — track clack, whistle and steam harmony, groan and squeak of weight and wood and iron. Children would stop rubbing their dusty feet against their calves, and something would tickle at the soles of men with lines etched deep in leathery brows. They would tuck their collars down to hide the frayed edges and straighten their ties. Women on the avenue gazed away into the air toward the train song, lost for a second, before the street light changed, calling them back.

Soon, her train would lumber heavily, growling and snorting, a curling dark line, from the cavernous station, and its song would meander, sad, thrilling, an indiscriminate version of love, into the nooks and crannies and hidden places where ordinary people lived.

But I, Josephine Lee, am not an ordinary one.

The whistle called again, and Jo's heart jerked against her ribs, her feet itching. She poked a finger into her shoe and rubbed, smiling to herself, then settled back into the plush, soft seat.

Edward finished shoving her valise into the overhead rack, and sat down beside his wife, across from Jo. Carl sat with her knees wide, her hands pushing her skirt down between her legs. "Give me a light, dear," she said. Edward sighed and reached into his pocket, but Jo was faster, the match flaring, cupped in her hand as Carl leaned forward. They grinned at each other, and Edward fluttered his hands in an exaggerated gesture of helplessness.

"You'll have to change," Carl reminded Jo again.

Jo shrugged and took off the suit jacket. "It's forever to Boston," she said, rolling up her sleeves, resting her ankle across her knee. They were rich, different, and Jo didn't know what part of her was this. *It will mark an empty place in me too. A place like "preacher's daughter," like "boy," like "girl," like "dyke," like " 'bo."*

Her nipples grazed the cool cloth of her shirt as she stretched her arm across the back of the seat, and she saw Carl glance at them and shake her head slightly to herself. "Neither boy nor girl," she muttered, tapping the ash from her thin cigar.

"Or maybe either." Edward laughed.

His eyes met Jo's and he sighed. "Those lashes..." He glanced out into the station. "That brother of yours."

"Gone home to be a preacher, foolish boy," laughed Carl. She flapped the skirt of her dress for air, and her eyes met Jo's. "He looked hard for you, you know."

Jo nodded, and something caught in her throat. She glanced down into the smoke of her cigarette. He had been to Hoovervilles all along the tracks since she'd left, tracking her from Miss Langley's directions North, and he'd spoken to Edward and to Max's mother, following her that night. "You're going to make your life hard," he had said to her. "Your family's life hard."

Max. Jo swallowed and looked away into the station.

"Don't you look the happy family," David said. He stuck his head through the door of the compartment, his hair slicked down, his collar bright against the scarlet bow tie. "Bags all stowed," he reported. He looked from one to the other of them, lips tight, eyes sharp and sparkling. "Hmm." He pointed to Carl and Edward, "Mother, Father ... or is it Father, Mother?" Carl rolled her eyes and blew a puff of smoke in his direction. Edward lifted up and pecked David's smooth clean cheek in a kiss. David looked at Jo. "And you? Sonny — or is it missy — going away to school?" He looked at Edward. "I thought you were going to get her into that lovely frock we bought."

Edward smiled and lifted his shoulders in a shrug. "Young people."

Jo smiled sadly, and watched her hands as Edward left to see David off the train. Maxine wanted family, to belong somewhere, *to belong to me.*

"You can change later," Carl said softly. "Again and again."

Something tapped at the window and Jo turned. *Max.* She started up from her seat, then hesitated.

Carl laughed. "Go on, she's waiting. We'll be at the Plaza in Boston if you miss the train. I'm sure you can find your way there alone."

Rain patted gently on the roof of the hollow baggage car in which Maxine and Jo had taken refuge just down the tracks from the station. "I just wanted to say goodbye," Maxine said softly, pulling her sweater close against the damp. The car lurched forward, and she smiled as Jo jerked around, saw that they were moving and then settled back against the wall.

"Guess this will get me to Boston as good as any other way."

She reached out and touched Jo's hand. "They're just moving it to a side track."

The silence rumbled and creaked with the swaying car. It stopped, then jerked forward and Maxine lurched sideways into Jo.

Jo groaned, stiff for only a second, then opened her eyes and kissed Maxine, pressing her mouth, as if their lips would bruise, against hers. Maxine settled again into the easy rocking of the car, feeling Jo's breath on her upper lip. Then she pushed herself quietly away. "No," she said. "This isn't where you belong."

Max's eyes were careful, the orange lashes damp, and Jo felt herself wanting to be still, stop moving, let the red head rest in the crook of her shoulder forever.

"You were right, yesterday," Max said. "You can't fold over some part of yourself and hide." She tried to smile. "Not you." Jo opened her mouth, wishing she could suck the words back in, wanting to protest that yes, she could, she did not need those empty spaces, those roads and marks, not all of them, but Max touched her fingers to her lips. "Don't."

She gathered her handbag, grasped her sweater close and stood up, swaying as the car reversed, rolling back into the siding. "Look at you," she said, smiling as Jo scrambled up next to her. "Like a man." She reached out and touched the sharp points of Jo's nipples, cupped the faint curve of her breasts. Jo shuddered. "But you don't hide . . . woman." She let her hand rest on the white of Jo's shirt, feeling the warmth and the heartbeat, then let it fall away.

"But I want you," Jo said finally. Her shoulders felt heavy, her back thin.

Tears slipped down Max's face. "You wouldn't be any good to me," she said. She gestured toward Jo's pants, her breasts. "This is danger. People will be angry. There's some who'll want to hurt you because they're afraid." She stopped and took a breath. "I'm afraid." Max looked away, her hand touching Jo's rolled sleeve. "I love you," she said, looking up again, "but you wouldn't be the same if you were the way I need . . ."

"Come with me then," Jo said, cocking her head toward a whistle as it screamed.

Maxine laughed, sniffing in her tears. "No." The car jerked again and stood still, and they heard the clank as the switchman released the buckle between cars. "I need a home," she said, nodding to herself. "I need to belong somewhere."

Jo caught herself as the engine lurched, pulling free.

Maxine swung down. Sam and Wit were waiting for her down the tracks. She looked back up at Jo, her legs spread wide, eyes bright and green, the hollow of the car dark behind her. "You," Maxine said, smiling. "You have places to go, places to be."

The hairs separated and fell away from the dirty blue ribbon, scattering into long lines over the onion-skin map, crossing boundaries, into familiar, strange lands. Jo brushed the strands aside, crumpled the map and tossed it into a trash bin. She leaned on the iron railing and looked down on the branching maze of silver rails, waiting for the next train. *New places to be.*

A family — a man, a woman, and a child — stood to her left. Jo smiled down at the girl. The little brow furrowed. She looked Jo up and down. Jo felt her suit and short hair acutely, her breasts obvious, her self clearly different. The little girl stared, then finally tugged on her mother's skirt until the woman looked down. The child pointed at Jo. "Mommy, is that a boy or a girl?"

The woman flushed and the man frowned. Jo bit her lip, then smiled again. The child looked back as her parents pulled her away.

Jo said it softly: "New places to be."

A few of the publications of
THE NAIAD PRESS, INC.
P.O. Box 10543 • Tallahassee, Florida 32302
Phone (904) 539-5965
Toll-Free Order Number: 1-800-533-1973
Mail orders welcome. Please include 15% postage.
Write or call for our free catalog which also features an
incredible selection of lesbian videos.

FORBIDDEN FIRES by Margaret C. Anderson. Edited by Mathilda
Hills. 176 pp. Famous author's "unpublished" Lesbian romance.
ISBN 1-56280-123-6 $21.95

SIDE TRACKS by Teresa Stores. 160 pp. Gender-bending
Lesbians on the road.   ISBN 1-56280-122-8   10.95

HOODED MURDER by Annette Van Dyke. 176 pp. 1st Jessie
Batelle Mystery.   ISBN 1-56280-134-1   10.95

WILDWOOD FLOWERS by Julia Watts. 208 pp. Hilarious and
heart-warming tale of true love.   ISBN 1-56280-127-9   10.95

NEVER SAY NEVER by Linda Hill. 224 pp. Rule #1: Never get involved
with . . .   ISBN 1-56280-126-0   10.95

THE SEARCH by Melanie McAllester. 240 pp. Exciting top cop
Tenny Mendoza case.   ISBN 1-56280-150-3   10.95

THE WISH LIST by Saxon Bennett. 192 pp. Romance through
the years.   ISBN 1-56280-125-2   10.95

FIRST IMPRESSIONS by Kate Calloway. 208 pp. P.I. Cassidy
James' first case.   ISBN 1-56280-133-3   10.95

OUT OF THE NIGHT by Kris Bruyer. 192 pp. Spine-tingling
thriller.   ISBN 1-56280-120-1   10.95

NORTHERN BLUE by Tracey Richardson. 224 pp. Police recruits
Miki & Miranda — passion in the line of fire.   ISBN 1-56280-118-X   10.95

LOVE'S HARVEST by Peggy Herring. 176 pp. by the author of
Once More With Feeling.   ISBN 1-56280-117-1   10.95

THE COLOR OF WINTER by Lisa Shapiro. 208 pp. Romantic
love beyond your wildest dreams.   ISBN 1-56280-116-3   10.95

These are just a few of the many Naiad Press titles — we are the oldest and
largest lesbian/feminist publishing company in the world. Please request a
complete catalog. We offer personal service; we encourage and welcome
direct mail orders from individuals who have limited access to bookstores
carrying our publications.